**And, before "The Swans of War",
there was
"The Lands That Lie Between"**

The day that Morgan lost her job, she knew that change was coming. She broke her lease, threw everything that she valued in life, including her cat Sam, into her van, kissed her adoptive family goodbye, and started a cross-country trek.

She knew that change was coming. She expected that.

What she wasn't expecting was elves, or magick walking in the world around her, or the beauty and danger of the Lands That Lie Between…

The Swans
of War

An Urban Fantasy
With Morgan and Sam

By Catherine Kane

Books by Catherine Kane

The Morgan and Sam urban fantasy series

The Lands That Lie Between

The Swans of War

Foresight Publications practical metaphysics

Adventures in Palmistry

The Practical Empath- Surviving and Thriving as a Psychic Empath

Manifesting Something Better: Easy, Quick and Fun Ways to Manifest the Life of Your Dreams

The Psychic Power of Your Dreams: Practical Skills for Working with Your Dreams for Insight, Information, Creativity and a Better Life

Magick for Pennies: Affordable Metaphysics for Everyone

Living in Interesting Times: Practical Energywork When Times Get Tough

The Swans
of War

An Urban Fantasy
With Morgan and Sam

By Catherine Kane

Foresight Publications
Wallingford, Ct

Table of Contents

The Magick Lies Right Besides Us

The lands of magick lie side by side with our everyday world, one step sideways from our reality. They're hard to see for those who do not have the eyes to see them.

A flash of color. A hint of mystery. A swift and sudden vision of that which we will not accept as being of our daily "real" world.

And so we block it out. We reason away the magick and the mystery, imprisoning it in "it must have been"s and "it couldn't be"s and all too reasonable explanations.

We miss the neighbors who are right beside us.

The lands of magick lie side by side with our everyday world, but they have other defenses besides the mortal eye's refusal to perceive them.

The lands of the Sidhe have gates – gates that only open in mortal lands at certain times and in certain places. Shifting, moving, melting into mist.

Unless you are a person with most peculiar powers, you shall not enter, save only at the appointed times and places. Indeed, for most mortals, even when the gates are open, the odds of wandering through are so slight as to be unfathomable.

Still, we mortals live cheek by jowl with magick every day.

One
Morning

Morgan smiled and briefly stretched her back and legs in the sunlight before beginning her morning qigong practice. The sounds of chimes and flute played gently in the background. The gradual increase in her reach and the flow of her movement felt good as her muscles relaxed into the discipline. She took a deep breath and emptied her mind of everything but the light and drawing that light into her new day.

Reach and stretch. Breathe. Gather light. Focus. Bring the light to center and down into the dantien; and pass through the movements once more. The rhythms of the discipline filling her with light and bringing her back to center.

As she came to the end of a round of movement, she caught a flash of gold from the corner of her eye. Smoothly ending the movement, she centered and turned to greet her roommate.

"Good morning, Sam" said Morgan.

The golden cat briefly struck a theatrical pose (and he was certainly worth looking at) before flowing into the room like water.

"Back at the morning workouts." he said. "Better you than me. It seems a shame to spoil a beautiful day by getting up into it so early."

Morgan grinned. "You're not fooling any one, you know" she said. "You train your muscles as hard or harder than I do. Anyone who takes more than a superficial look at you can tell that; and you've been up for hours, padding around about your business. Next to you, I'm just a rank beginner."

A smile crept across Sam's furry face. "Ah well, I

do the best I can" he said.

"And you, you're getting a lot better" he rushed on. "I've been watching you. Your breath and endurance is increasing, you're getting stronger and more flexible, your reflexes are much better."

"In short, I'm in much better shape. Just in case I ever have to run for my life again." Morgan twinkled at him. "I might even be able to land a totally wild punch or two, if I really needed to."

Their eyes met, in perfect understanding.

"But, enough of this sweet talk" said Sam. "By the clock on the wall, I'd say it's just about time for second breakfast. Last one to the kitchen is bane's bait."

The cat darted quickly out of the room, with the woman in hot pursuit.

Two
Unseelie Plotting

In a darker corner of the lands that lie between, things were not as pleasant.

The power had passed from past court to present in the previous fall. The Seelie court had retained its ascendance and held the upper hand in both the lands that lie between and the mundane land they were connected with.

The Unseelie lord sneered and took another sip of his wine. That was not what should have happened. Plans had been made. Actions had been taken. Lesser lights of the Seelie had been eliminated to tip the scales in favor of Unseelie powers.

And somehow, it had not been enough, and the Seelie now ruled the lands. Again.

He sat in his darkened workroom, amidst ancient books and items of power and far less savory things, brooding and drinking. It should not have happened.

His jaw tightened. He was going to change things.

He put his cup aside and closed his eyes in contemplation. A direct assault had not worked. Perhaps he needed something more convoluted. A bit more subtle.

Minutes passed; and then slowly, slowly, an unpleasant smile crept across his handsome features.

Yes. That might do it.

And if it did not, he would lose nothing.

He stood and began his preparations.

Three
The Taking of the Swan Princess

The bright young cygnet maiden, as fair as any spring flower, rode forth amidst the morning dew, with her ever-present guards close at her heels. Ariella was her mother's greatest treasure, and like any treasure, her mother did her best to hold her tight and keep her safe from harm.

But safety can be a suffocation, especially when you are young and beautiful and know but little of the world. The young princess was tired of her guards. Tired of their closeness and concern for her. Tired of safety.

And so, she laughed and spurred her horse and forged ahead, catching her watchful companions by surprise.

How she laughed at the looks of alarm on their faces, as they urged their steeds to follow hers. She was still laughing as she rode forwards into the trap.

Weapons flashed. Metal clanged. Men cried out in pain and fear.

And the girl was pulled down viciously from her horse and thrown across another. Saw motionless bodies littering the ground, as she was borne away, out of the safety of the life she knew,

And into the wild beyond.

Four
Breakfast at Morgan's and Sam's

In the kitchen, piles of bagels, cream cheese and heaps of smoked salmon were laid out on pretty stoneware plates, next to a tall carafe of chilled juice. The newspaper was laid out as well, thoughtfully folded open to the local news. The spirit of their hearth had evidently been hard at work.

"What a lovely breakfast set-up" said Morgan. "Aren't we lucky to have it?"

There was no formal reply from the hearth spirit, but, at once, the room felt slightly sunnier and more friendly.

"And I wonder who picked up the house, took out the trash and started a load of laundry last night after some of us were in bed." said Morgan. "It's a shame that I can't thank them for all of the help."

A faint giggling drifted in from the living room that they had just left.

"Well, fine." said the cat sardonically. "You know you're not supposed to acknowledge the presence of brownies, because if you do, they might get offended and leave. Just go ahead and mess with thousands of years of tradition. Why they don't leave you flat for gags like that is beyond me." The giggling got louder. "Go ahead" he mock-snarled. "Encourage her. You'll only give her a swelled head and who knows what she'll be up to next."

He scowled, but then his face brightened.

"Ooooo, lox!" he added more cheerfully, hooking out a double portion for himself with one extended claw.

Morgan grabbed for the plate quickly, knowing that, if she didn't nail down her salmon now, her bagel would be fish free this morning. A few minutes later, the bagel spread with butter and cream cheese with a beautiful slice of salmon

9

to top it off and a cold cup of juice in hand, Morgan settled down to the news of her little corner of the world, with Sam peering interestedly over her shoulder.

"There's a lecture at the library this evening on simple stress relief" said Morgan. "That's good. I'd like to drop by and say hello to Mary. And a sale on exercise shoes at Casuals- I'll have to stop by next week."

"Look at that" Sam said, pawing the bottom edge of the page. "Seems there's been a big problem lately with small critters in the west end of town. Lots of folks being invaded by vermin that never had a problem before."

"I can't believe the odd things that interest you" said Morgan, lovingly rubbing his ears.

Sam purred for a moment, then opened one eye.

"Yeah, well, I'm a cat, and cats find small rodents interesting. It's in our job description."

"As if I could possibly ever forget that you're a cat." said Morgan, laughing. "Well, I'd better get ready for work. Any particular page you want the paper left at?"

Sam quickly scanned the rest of the local news. "You could leave it opened to the national news" he said "and this time, leave the television remote where I can get at it. I almost broke my neck getting it off of the armoire last week."

"I'll be stopping off at Good Energy on my way home from work" Morgan called as she stood and walked into the other room. "I thought I'd get a hug from Sara and see if there's anything else there I can't live without. Is there anything you need?"

"Not there," answered Sam "but, if you could happen to stop by the market afterwards, we've just officially run out of salmon."

There was a long and ominous silence from the other room.

Five
Bound

They had taken her fine cloak of feathers from her, so she could not transform herself and fly.

They had bound her arms and legs securely, so she could not run.

And, tired of her raging and shouting, they had gagged her mouth so she could not scream.

Huddled deeply into the corner where they had dropped her, Ariella watched her captors, wide eyed in the dim light, and wondered what they had planned for her...

Six
Good Energy

At the end of her work day, Morgan went by her local new age shop, Good Energy. The door chimes jingled melodiously as she gently pushed the door open, stopping for a moment to drink in the serenity of the shop.

Sara stopped crocheting and waved enthusiastically at her from behind the counter. "How's it going?" the motherly woman chirped at Morgan. "Are those meditation CDs working for creating a more tranquil, stress free home situation; or are they just relaxing you so much that you want to take a nap? For me, I found it took me time to figure out the right soundscape for balance between tranquility and comatose."

"Yes." answered Morgan. "Thanks for asking. I'm finding bird song is helpful but a little light, but the wind in the trees recording makes me feel relaxed without nodding off. Next time, I'll have to add the stream to my collection. This time though, I've dropped in for some time with your tarot reader, and a hug from you, of course. After all, they've done medical studies that show that having a lot of hugs is essential for a person's health, haven't they?"

Sara's eyes twinkled. "They certainly have. Medical science is finally catching up to things that more sensible people have known for generations, and, I can certainly fill that order for you now." she said, laying down her latest project and coming around the counter.

Morgan stepped into her open arms and hugged her back. She'd always enjoyed hugs from people she liked, but there was something special about Sara's hugs that made her feel stronger, calmer, and happier. Whenever she went by "Good Energy", a hug from Sara was always an essential part of the visit.

She smiled. "Thanks" she said. "That always makes my day." Sara gave her an extra squeeze, and then opened her arms and stood back from Morgan, looking at her more intently.

"I'm seeing you've got other business here besides just hugs' she said "and more things coming to you than you know yet. You'd best get at it then."

Morgan laughed.

"There's always something coming down the road." she said. "Is he ready for me yet?"

Sara withdrew behind the counter.

"Go on back" she said, returning to her crocheting. "He's been waiting for you."

Morgan headed for the back of the store, distracted on the way by beautiful and curious things recently put out on display. Despite the many tempting diversions, she eventually arrived at the private reading room behind the curtain deep in the recesses of the store.

The tarot reader was sitting there, peering down at the cards laid out on the table before him. He was tall and strong looking, with flowing grey hair, an energetic mustache and beard, a tattoo, an earring and kind eyes. In his denim vest with the runes on the back, he looked like Santa Claus, the biker years.

"It's nice to see you again." he said, smiling. "How are those wards I set on your new place doing?"

"Quite well, actually" she answered. "We haven't had an incursion of Unseelie pests or eldritch powers for several months now. I must say I'm glad of that. The "powers of darkness" are hard on my carpets."

"I'm so glad that I asked you about that, though. I'd never heard about wards until you told me about them; and they make perfect sense to me. If you can physically lock your doors, you'd surely want a way to meta – physically

14

lock them."

"Yeah, well, it's a wonder to me that more people don't know about simple things like wards." he said thoughtfully. "It's basic metaphysics to protect your space from negative things and energy; and it's commonly known in pagan and some other metaphysical circles. For some reason, though, while the literature and media are full of information about love spells, seeing auras and manifesting large amounts of cash in your spare time, the simple groundwork of magick, like warding your space to keep out things you don't want to come in and keep in things you don't want to get out, is basic information that somehow doesn't circulate. That's how a lot of new practitioners get hurt."

"Anyone with even a touch of talent can cast a circle and call up wards; and anyone with a lick of sense will do so, especially if they're energetically sensitive or tend to receive calls from things that go bump in the night." he continued.

"Anyone can do it?" asked Morgan, surprised.

"Sure can." he said. "From what I've seen, most people have at least a touch of the Gift in them. The problem is that such gifts aren't generally accepted in the world that we live in today. This means that, for most folks, as far as they know, there's no one to tell them they have a gift, no one to say that such gifts are normal, and no one to teach them how to use that gift safely and ethically. You can't even begin to gain any ability or control in a skill if you don't know it exists, can you now?"

He smiled a bit at the look of surprise on her face.

"Just as an example' he said, picking up a long length of chain with a crystal at the bottom. He held it up so the crystal was dangling.

"Show me "yes", please" he said. The pendulum began to gently swing forwards and back.

"Now, show me "no", please." he said. It paused, and then switched direction, swinging left and right.

"Now, you try it" he said, holding the pendulum out to her.

She took it gingerly, holding it between her thumb and forefinger.

"Show me "yes", please" she said formally.

And the pendulum began to swing forwards and back...

Her eyes went wide.

"Is that me doing that?" she asked.

"Maybe you," he smiled. "Maybe it's your higher self or a guardian spirit. The point is that it's that little spark of talent inside of you that lets you tap into knowledge like this."

"But it's just swinging back and forth" she said. "That's not really such a big deal."

"By itself, no," he answered, "but with a little practice, you can use it to answer questions, find lost things, tap into higher knowledge and do a bundle of other interesting things."

"Can you show me how?" she asked.

"Well, sure" he said "but first you're going to want a pendulum of your own. This one goes forwards and back for yes, and side to side for no; but other pendulums may use the opposite movements, or even circles to give you those yes/ no answers. Some pendulums even have different sets of "Yes /No" s for different people. You always need to start out with the "show me" exercises with a new pendulum to find out exactly how it says yes and no for you."

"Sara has a great assortment of pendulums up front." he said. "Go find the one that's right for you, then come on back and I'll show you how to use it."

Morgan hurried to the front of the shop to the display of pendulums. Beautiful crystals, pieces of turned wood, and bits of interesting metal on long chains glistened in the afternoon sun, and she found her hand drawn to a mottled green one.

Morgan held the pendulum up carefully. "Show me yes, please" she said.

And the moss agate pendulum slowly, slow-ly began to swing forwards and back…

Seven
Cruelty and Deception

The first step of the Unseelie lord's plan was all but complete. And now to lay more merry mischief.

He had locked the princess' feather cloak away very carefully, lest, in a moment of distraction, she seized upon it and made her escape. He brought it out now and, heavily crossing the room in the dim light, placed it down; near–to-hand but not close enough for her to touch it, bound as she was.

Drawing out his long knife, he held it a moment. Then he drew it slowly, painfully, across the outside of her bound arm, marking her soft and snowy skin.

He smiled. He liked his work.

Behind her gag, he heard her hiss with pain, but not cry out.

"Proud, and brave" he thought. "For now, at least."

Seizing the cloak, he deliberately rubbed it back and forth across the bleeding. Slowly. Mottling it with her blood.

The princess stared at him defiantly and did not cry.

When his task was finally done to his satisfaction, he arose, taking the bespoiled feather cloak with him, as he walked across the room to the door.

He had places to go…

People to fool…

Wars to start…

Eight
Swan Knight

They had ridden forth as usual, following in the train of the princess Ariella. Watching her. Guarding her. Riding close upon her dainty heels.

He had ridden behind her, ridden amongst the close press of his fellow warriors. They were considered to be the best of the best, the strongest and fiercest warriors handpicked for this very special assignment to guard the daughter of the leader of their flock.

The young cob felt proud to be one of them.

They had ridden forth as usual, following in the train of the delicate princess. Watching her. Guarding her.

And she had merrily spurred her horse forwards. Laughing as she rode towards freedom. Ahead of them- just for an instant.

And then, disaster struck.

Dark figures rising out of the underbrush. Flying darts and brandished swords. A sudden and violent impact to the back of his head, and the world swimming around him. Toppling from his saddle and hitting the ground hard, as his companions fell around him.

Seeing the princess wrest from her saddle and thrown across the back of a mount with eyes like flame. Hearing her cry out as she was borne away.

Darkness falling.

He awoke in the gathering dusk. In a pool of his own blood. His feather cloak missing.

With the bodies of his friends lying stark and still around him.

Weak and dizzy, he struggled to his knees and

crawled from figure to figure, hoping in vain that someone, anyone was alive besides him.

He was alone.

There was no one left but him to let the swan folk know what had happened to their princess and her warriors. No one but he to bear the word and set the people on her track.

And he was still faint and bleeding…

Swearing, crying, he tore strips from his tunic and bound his wounds up as best he could, trying to staunch the flow of blood. Pulling to his feet, he looked around, and found the horses all fled.

Swearing again, he began to stagger in a direction that he hoped would bring him to some kind of sanctuary and help in time. If his wounds did not take him first.

In the distance, he heard the sound of howling. Suddenly chilled, he found that he could move faster than he had thought that he could.

Nine
False Clue

It was near the place where the princess had been taken captive and her guards cut down– but not too near, as its falling was meant to seem an accident. It was partially concealed amongst the growing brush– but not too well concealed as he wanted it easily found. And it was in the direction that led directly towards one of the gateways opening unto the Seelie court.

The Unseelie lord bent down and carefully placed the bloody cloak of swan feathers on the ground, half hidden by a dark and spiny bush. Beside it, just as carefully, he placed a metal brooch with closure pin half twisted into a broken mass. A brooch worn only by the high rulers and leaders of the Seelie court.

Standing up, he carefully surveyed his handiwork.

He dug in with his heels, leaving multiple scuff marks and the illusion of a scuffle as if someone had tried to break away from a captor. He led his horse by repeatedly, leaving tracks as of that of a warrior band. He broke branches and weeds, to further the impression of a violent struggle.

Standing up once more, he took stock of his illusion and the story it told.

He smiled briefly. He really did enjoy his work.

But not everyone was going to.

He led his horse carefully away over such rocks as he could find, so his going was concealed and the only tracks led towards the Seelie gate.

And cloak and brooch lay together in the stillness- awaiting the searchers yet to come.

Ten
Tarot

"Now I believe that you were here for a tarot reading." said the grey-haired reader as Morgan watched the pendulum swing to and fro. "Is there are a particular question or area of concern you have in mind, or do you just want a general reading?"

Morgan blinked and returned her focus to the reason she had come in the first place. "I'm not quite sure." she began hesitantly. "Things have been going well. Very well, in fact, but I've got this slightly unsettled feeling, kinda like the air before a storm rolls in. No reason. Indeed, every reason to feel relaxed – but I don't."

"So, I guess I'm here for an outside view- to see if this is just stress or if there's something to this uneasy feeling." she said.

"We can do that" said the tarot reader "and, given your history, I think it's worth paying attention to your instincts and double checking them when you're moved to. First, though, let's review the basics about readings and what they can really do for you, just so we avoid any self-fulfilling prophecies."

"It's important to keep in mind" he said "that you have this thing called Free will. That means you can make choices and have a certain amount of control over your life by the choices you make. Because of that, you don't have just one future. You have many, and, at any time, you can choose to change the direction of your life and head off into a new one."

He picked up the tarot deck and shuffled the cards.
"Any good reading" he said "tells you where you're heading in life if you keep doing what you're doing- but you can always change directions. At that point, if you hear

something in a reading you don't like, that can be helpful. It lets you know it may be time to look at your life and see if you need to change your approach."

"Does that make sense? he said, looking her straight in the eye. She thought a minute and nodded.

"Then we're ready to go." he said and placed the cards on the table before her. "Cut the cards," he said "just no cartoon type cuts using battle axes."

She grinned and cut the cards, and the reader stacked them and began to lay them out on the table between them.

"We start with the Fool." he said.

Her eyes narrowed. "Are the cards calling me names?" she said

The reader laughed "No, the Fool is the symbol for someone at the start of their journey. They don't know everything, but they are brave and willing to learn. They just need to be sure to watch their step as they go on their way."

"Next, we have the card that crosses you, the obstacle you must overcome." He turned the card over and frowned. "We see the Lightning Struck Tower. Things go to pieces, in a sudden and possibly violent way. You'll have to be ready to adjust."

"The foundation of the situation" he said, drawing a third card "is Judgement, which, in this case, says that issues you thought dead and buried return, but you'll have the opportunity to put them to bed for good. The next two cards" he said, laying them out "say that good things you've done in the past will lead to help in your present situation, and that help will also come from new and unexpected sources. "

"The sixth card, the Star, is a card says that, to obtain what you want, you will have to face the things you fear."

"That's a lot of trump cards…" he said with concern in his eyes. "Sounds like you've got some challenging times on the way."

Eleven
...And One Still Lives...

Without her feather cloak, the cold bit into her arms and legs like icy teeth. She drew herself into a tiny ball as best as her bonds would let her, hiding from the cold and from her situation, trying to hold inside her what warmth she could.

She heard the door creak open in the front room as one of her captors returned.

"Did you catch up with him?" one of his fellows asked him.

Her heart leapt within her. Had one of her guards escaped? Which one? Who was still alive?

"No." the first one snarled. "The swan boy was moving too fast for us to us to catch him right away. But it is only a matter of time. He is leaking like a sieve and leaving a clear trail for the hounds to follow; and, given the amount of blood he is losing, I do not think that he has much time left."

"And he is miles away from any help, as well. There is no question about it – we will settle with him before he does the boss' plan any harm."

In the other room, a tear ran down her cheek.

Her guards- all were dead, save for only one.

And he would surely die soon.

All because of her foolishness.

The swan princess stifled her sobs and turned her mind to trying her best to stay alive and try to escape.

Twelve
The Tree of Life

"…Sounds like your instincts were right. You've got some challenging times on the way." he said.

Morgan nodded tensely. She remembered what the previous challenging times had been like.

"But don't worry yet." he added quickly. "Remember, you have free will so you have the ability to change the direction of your life. Knowing there are obstacles on the way puts you in a better position to deal with them or dodge them altogether."

"Fortunately, that's not all the reading has to tell us. Let's do the second half and see what more it has to say."

"Now we start up the tree of life" he said, beginning the second part of the reading. "This first card says the situation is about deception and truth, and that you'll be called upon to shine the light that illuminates the truth and reveals deception."

"The second card speaks of your hopes and fears. Though you may have doubts, it's important to believe in yourself and your ability to do what needs to be done."

"The third card talks about how others see you. It says that, while others may see you according to their own beliefs, you need to be true to your true self, not who they think you are."

"And the final card, the Sun, says that you will prevail if you hang in there and do the best you can."

The tarot reader looked across the table at her. "It sounds like things are going to get wild for a while, and things will not be easy or comfortable; but it also sounds like you won't have to go it alone and that you'll be getting help when you least expect it. The important thing here seems to believe than you can, and just keep going."

29

He smiled kindly at her "Given how you came through your last adventure, that somehow doesn't surprise me. Now do you have any questions or concerns that you need clarified?"

Morgan was still tense, but she found herself relaxing slightly. be that you can handle this if you think on your feet and

"Everything" she said "but I think I'm going to have to go think about this before I figure out what other questions to ask. The important parts are to know that there's a reason I've been uneasy, to be ready for when things start to change and to know that, even if things get scary, there's a good chance that I'll make it through this and out the other side if I can only keep my wits around me. The rest I'll have to figure out as I go along."

"If you need help, you know where to find me." he said. "Just call my number for advice or for backup, and I'll do what I can."

"Thanks" said Morgan, sliding his card in her pocket "and thanks for the reading, too. This may be the heads up that I need to make things work."

She opened her purse to pull out the payment for her reading, placing it carefully in his singing bowl. She nodded to him once before standing and walking away. Evidently, there were bumps on the road ahead and she needed to get ready.

Thirteen
Captivity

Rough voices echoed from the front room.

"It is time to move her royal highness" one growled. "Move her to where no one will be able to find her."

Another voice tittered unpleasantly. "Should not want to be her." it said. "Once a sorcerer gets his hands on you, there is no telling what might happen."

Footsteps came creaking across the floor and the door squealed open. She'd been in the dark back room for quite some time now, and blinked at the unaccustomed light, tears forming at the corners of her eyes.

"You are a pretty one" said the first voice, face masked by the glare. "If I did not have my orders concerning you..."

The swan maid shuddered.

"But you do," broke in the second voice "so we had best be moving on. Bind her eyes, so she cannot see where we will be taking her."

A worn, stained and smelly band of cloth covered her eyes and was tied firmly behind her head. The loss of sight only emphasized the hopelessness of the situation she was in.

Bound, blind, gagged, the swan princess was swung over a massive shoulder and carried away like she was nothing.

Fourteen
An Unexpected Visitor...

Later in the evening, Sam was sitting on the sofa watching T.V. while Morgan was rummaging around in the other room.

"Did you find your car keys yet?" called out Sam from the couch.

"Not yet." answered Morgan, still searching. After a few minutes, she stood up and looked around, baffled. The keys were in none of the places she could think of.

She thought for a moment. Slowly, hesitantly, she went to her purse and pulled out the pendulum that she'd bought that afternoon.

"Are my car keys in this room?" she asked quietly, and held the pendulum suspended in the air. The pendulum began to swing in the direction that she'd learned was its special "yes". She'd seen it work that afternoon, but the hairs still stirred slightly on the back of her neck.

She mentally divided the room into quarters. "Are they in this quarter?" she asked. The answer came back "no".

"This quarter?" she asked, indicating another quarter. The answer came back "yes".

"Show me where" she said and started moving slowly through the room. As she did so, the pendulum began to swing, and, following the swing, she gradually homed in on a particular armchair. When she brought the pendulum over the chair, the pendulum moved once more and then stopped dead.

Reaching down, Morgan fumbled around under the cushions. In less than a minute, she felt the runaway keys.

"Wow," Morgan breathed. The pendulum moved in the "yes" direction for a moment, seemingly in response to what she'd said.

Morgan watched it, and then said "Well, thank you." The pendulum danced about in a circle for a few seconds, and then went still. Morgan blinked and then tucked the pendulum away carefully before going into the other room.

"Find them?" asked Sam, his golden eyes fixed on the T.V. screen.

Morgan jingled the keys in her hand and sat down companionably with Sam on the couch, scratching him behind his fuzzy golden ears. She pulled the couch blanket around her shoulders against the evening chill, and Sam cuddled up in the warm and cozy space beside her.

"Do you think those girls ever heard of wards?" asked Sam, indicating the television with one paw. "This is the fourth week in a row that something powerful and evil has just materialized in their house without so much as a "by your leave".

"I think it's due to a limited budget for sets." grinned Morgan. "I guess it's probably less expensive to rebuild and destroy the same set every week than it is to create a new one every time."

"Well, it may be economically sound, but, frankly, magick doesn't **work** that way" whined Sam, his ears flattening slightly. "There are rules. There are procedures. There are the basic things that every little wood spirit and kitchen witch learns at the very beginning of her education, the kind of basic stuff that keep this kind of garbage from happening to them. It's the equivalent of a first time cook learning not to touch a hot stove!"

"I know, I know," soothed Morgan "but they don't know any better. It's only Hollywood magick. They probably don't have an actual metaphysical consultant anywhere near as magnificent as you on call."

"They call themselves witches." snorted Sam. "They might as well hang a big red sign on their front porch saying

"Evil beings- inquire within. All you can eat buffet". <u>And</u> install a revolving door beside the sign."

Just then, they heard a heavy crash on the front porch.

Sam looked at Morgan. Morgan looked at Sam.

"Interesting timing." said Sam.

Morgan got up quickly off of the couch and headed for the door.

"Just a minute there, girlfriend." said Sam, jumping down and bounding forwards to land between her and the door frame.

Pushing past the alerted cat, Morgan peered through the peep hole that she'd made sure was installed as soon as they had moved in. Squinting through the peep hole, she saw the face of a man that she had never seen before. He was tall, blond and had eyes of deep cerulean blue. And, by the scratches and bruises that covered his face, he was also in trouble.

Big trouble.

As she watched, his eyes rolled up in his head, and he collapsed out of her line of sight.

Her hand went to the door knob.

"Wait just a minute there" repeated Sam. "You're going to do it. You're going to open that door, aren't you?"

Morgan nodded. "There's someone out there in trouble." she blurted. "We can't just leave him out there."

In the distance, something howled. Woman and cat froze for a second.

"Right. There's someone out there in trouble. Well, there may well be someone in here in trouble in a minute," snorted Sam. "and I've got a really bad feeling that it's gonna be us."

Seeing her stricken face, his tone softened. "I know, I know- you've gotta be who you are. And who you are is someone who can't see someone in trouble without trying to

35

help them. You open the door if you have to, girl. Just be careful and be ready to close it again fast if you need to. I've got your back."

Heart in her mouth and hand on the door knob, she turned the knob and cautiously pulled the door open.

Outside, in the fading light of the day, a massive figure sprawled across the porch. Blond and muscular, dressed in leather, linen, and fur, he looked like an extra from some funky Viking movie. If it weren't for the bruises and blood covering his arms, head and torso, Morgan might have thought this was some kind of bad joke.

Sam took a sharp breath beside her. "A Swan Knight! Damn!" he said.

And then they heard the howling again. Closer now.

The blond man groaned and their eyes shot back to him. He opened his eyes and tried to pull himself to a sitting position, but collapsed on the porch again, exhausted from the effort.

"Please..." he said. "...help..."

His eyes slid closed once more and his body went limp as he passed out. A pool of blood formed around him, beginning to spread across the porch as they watched.

Morgan took a deep breath, bent over, grasped the blond man by the wrists and began to pull.

"Are you nuts?" gasped Sam. "I've audited an online first aid course. You shouldn't just drag someone around who's injured like this."

"...Unless I find him in a dangerous area..." replied Morgan, continuing to pull. "...and I think that this just might qualify for that..."

Multiple approaching howls in the twilight punctuated her statement.

"Are you crazy?" said Sam again. "This guy is a swan knight. A **swan knight!** They're flipping dangerous."

"Doesn't look too dangerous to me." said Morgan, continuing to haul, "and if we don't get him inside quickly, he's going to be an ex- swan knight! Now, will you hush up and help me here?"

"For the love of Mike!" said Sam. "How do I get myself into these things?"

He set his teeth into a relatively convenient leather strap and began to pull as well, leaning all of his weight into it.

Inch by inch, bit by bit, they dragged the heavy man across the porch and through the door as the sun sank in the sky and the ominous sounds grew closer.

"Blood trail." Morgan thought frantically as the stranger's feet crossed the threshold. "The blood will let them know where he is." She dashed to the closet where she kept the cleaning supplies, grabbing a mop and squirt bottle of cleaning solution with bleach. She ran back to the porch and started scrubbing furiously, erasing the trail of blood their unconscious guest had left while Sam kept an uneasy watch.

Minutes later, porch clean, shining and reeking of bleach and pine as if nothing untoward had ever happened there, Morgan and Sam retreated behind the heavy door themselves, shutting it and locking it tightly.

"I hope that those wards hold." said Sam nervously.

Morgan turned to the blond man on the floor, kneeling by his side and inspecting him more closely. His face was pale and his eyes were closed. Cuts and bruises covered his arms, his legs, his face, his body. A large wound gaped open on his chest and a smaller one on the side of his head; the sources of the blood he'd left as they moved him.

"Sam, I need the first aid kit." said Morgan, grabbing a blanket from a nearby chair, and pressing it firmly to the man's chest wound to try to staunch the flow of blood.

"On it!" the golden cat replied, leaping swiftly towards the bathroom closet. He returned in a minute, the white plastic kit clenched in his teeth.

Morgan replaced the blanket with a stack of gauze pads, strapping them firmly in place with surgical tape. The head wound was bleeding more slowly, so she briefly took the time to disinfect it before bandaging it as well. Then, she pulled back the blond man's tunic to check for additional wounds.

As she worked, she heard the sound of the cleaner squirt bottle being used behind her.

"Sam…" she said carefully, her fingers still busy with disinfectant and bandages "…how are you using a squirt bottle? You have no thumbs."

"Well, there are some Mysteries of Cats that man was not meant to wot of," he answered "but the truth is that the brownies are taking care of things."

There was the sound of giggling behind her and the smell of bleach filled the air.

The pad on the blond man's chest began to redden, as blood seeped through it. Positioning herself carefully, Morgan applied direct pressure to the wound to slow the blood loss.

The sudden sound of a heavy body climbing onto the porch froze her in mid action.

Sam looked at Morgan. Morgan looked at Sam. Both of them held their breath.

They could hear the sound of a second massive form joining the first. Then a third. Then the sound of sniffing, as of several **things** casting about for a scent.

The blond man stirred and began to moan.

There was a sudden silence on the porch – the intense silence of something or things listening hard.

Wide eyed, Morgan clapped one over her patient's

mouth to quiet him, while her other hand continued to try to stop the bleeding.

There was the sound of heavy bodies moving. Slinking towards the front door.

The sound of s–c–r–a–t–c–h–i–n–g of claws against the door panels. Down and up, to the height of a tall man's reach.

Once.

Twice.

A third time.

And then, a crashing blow struck violently against the heart of the door- and the door answered with a thunderous blast and a burst of brilliant light.

A violent howling sprang up on the porch, a howling full of pain and rage and suffering. Bodies thrashed about, striking out wildly, and more bursts of light and sound rose up in response.

With a rush and a snarl and a final chorus of baying, the porch was empty once more.

Morgan and Sam paused for a long moment, awaiting further onslaughts. Hearing none, they relaxed.

"Remind me to thank the guy who put those wards in." said Sam, only half flippantly.

Morgan looked down. The stranger's bleeding seemed to have stopped. The eyes of the blond man were open, and there was an awareness in them that had not been there before. She removed the hand she'd placed over his mouth.

"Please" he said. "help…I …need..."

"Stay still" said Morgan. "You've been badly hurt, and you need to lie still or you'll start bleeding again."

"No…" he said, trying to sit up. "help…I…need."

"You're safe, dear" said Morgan. "We've hidden you, and whatever accursed things were following you have gone away, so you're o.k., at least for now. But you really do need to lie still. You're in bad shape here, and if you don't stay still, you're going to start your wounds bleeding again"

"That's right" said Sam, from out of the man's field of vision. "Struggle around, and your bleeding will mess up her recently cleaned foyer, and it ain't gonna do you much good either."

"No.." said the blond man urgently. "Understand you do not. The princess taken vas. Of her guards, the only one living I am. Our chieftainess, I must tell."

Pushing her away, he tried to sit up. When he was only half way upright, his face turned deadly pale. He held his position for a moment, and then dropped to the floor once more. His eyes closed, and he passed out.

Silently, Morgan checked his pulse and breathing. His pulse was elevated but steady and his breathing was shallow, but present. Her visitor was in bad shape but would probably live the night. He was a bit too big for her to get up off the floor by herself, though.

Morgan looked up at Sam. Sam scowled.

"Swan princess too?" said Sam. "Well, that just opens up a whole new world of trouble."

Morgan sighed. "It does, eh?" she said. "Well, you just wait until I make our new guest a bit more comfortable, and then I think that you'd better fill me in on everything you know about these swan people."

Climbing back to her feet, she went to the linen closet to get blankets and pillows to keep her patient warm and more comfortable on the floor for the night. Staying warm would make it easier for his body to heal and prevent shock.

For that matter, she thought, she really ought to get enough bedding to keep herself comfortable too. She'd need to camp out in the front hall herself tonight, to stay close enough to monitor him in case he took a turn for the worse.

It was going to be a long night tonight, she thought, and she had the uneasy feeling that this was only the start of things to come.

Fifteen
Storytime

It took a while to get their unexpected guest tucked in and then to settle herself in a comfy chair in the hall, wrapped in a quilt and ready to monitor him as needed.

Morgan turned her attention to her cat.

"Alright, Sam" she said briskly. "It's clear you know more about what's going on here than I do; so, spill it. What's a swan knight and why should I be worried about having one collapsed on the floor in my front hall?"

Sam hesitated and cleared his throat. "A swan knight..." he said. "Um, er, a swan knight is...oh, I'd better just start at the beginning! When you were a little girl, you probably heard the story of the six swan princes and their brave sister, right?"

"I'm not sure," said Morgan. "Give me a refresher."

Sam paused and settled himself in a more formal position. "Well, long ago and far away," he said in a sing song voice. "There was once a man with six sons and a beautiful daughter whose wife had died (as it so often goes in these kinds of stories.) When he remarried, his new wife seemed to love his children, but, in truth, resented them for the hold that they had on his heart."

"One day, when her husband was away on a trading expedition, she took her stepchildren far into the wilds of the back country in the marshes. Once she had them thoroughly lost and turned around, she revealed her true nature and cast a curse upon the boys, condemning them to spend the rest of their lives trapped in the forms of swans. They would only be able to return to their actual human forms once at the end of six years. Their sister could save them from the curse, but only if she made six shirts out of nettles, remaining totally silent while she did so. Throwing the six finished shirts over

43

her brothers' heads at the end of their six years would lift the curse, but only if their sister could keep her silence throughout the entire process."

"Then, laughing, their evil stepmother left them there, and returned to her home, telling their father that his children were ungrateful and had run away. And why not laugh? She had set a truly wicked curse, filled with impossible tasks for its unwinding."

"The swans honked piteously, and then spread their wings and leapt into the skies. Their sister bit her lip and went to work, gathering the nettles she needed to save her brothers. She gathered the nettles, cleaned and prepared them and spun them bit by bit into the thread that she needed to weave the fabric for each shirt in turn. The nettles stang terribly and her fingers bled as she worked with them, and not a word could she say as she worked, for a single word would end her chances of breaking the curse and doom her six brothers to live forever as swans."

"And she found that it took an entire year to make each nettle shirt."

"Four years and more passed in spinning and in silence."

"One day, a king went riding in the marshes, looking for new and interesting things to hunt. He saw great swans in the distance, larger and more noble than any bird or beast that he had ever seen before. When he followed the flight of the swans, he came to an island in the midst of the fens, and, upon the island sat a beautiful woman, spinning upon a hand spindle."

"Looking upon her, he felt his heart leap within him, and he was struck with love for her. "Fair maiden" he said (for the colors of her distaff ribbons told him that she was indeed a maiden.) "Your beauty has captured my heart. I am a king, but before you, I am as nothing. Speak to me, that I may hear a voice as lovely as your face."

"The woman opened her mouth, then paused, and shook her head sadly. She gestured to her mouth and shook her head again."

"The king said "You cannot speak? A very sad thing, but still I find myself drawn to you in love. Will you be my bride? Will you leave this dismal swamp, marry me and live together with me in my palace?""

"The woman paused a moment, thought about it, and nodded her head yes. She gathered up all of the nettles, the thread that she had spun and other things necessary to her task. The king swept her up on to the back of his noble charger, and together they rode out of the swamp, into the sunset and back to the palace, where they were married with due ceremony after an appropriate amount of time."

"And despite his total sappiness" said Sam "The king turned out to be a good husband, too - kind and respectful and loving. And the sister of the swan cursed brothers came to truly love him as well. And within a short time, it became clear that the king and his silent mysterious queen were with child. And they were happy together."

"But not every one else was."

"The king's mother had become very fond of the power she gained from being the only woman in her son's life. She was not at all pleased that he had wed this silent woman that he had found in the midst of a swamp known for enchantment."

"This woman could be anything- anything at all. A witch, a spirit, a curse bound in human form. After all, no natural woman could possibly keep her peace for so long a time."

"And now she had power over the young king, and he would not hear a word against her."

"The queen mother convinced herself that a great evil was happening here. And she set about watching for a way to free her son from his obsession."

"The young queen had been given a tower room for her own delight, and there had set up a massive loom by the light from the eastern window. And there she stayed, from sun up to sun down, spinning the nettles into yarn, then threading her loom and weaving the prickly yarn into cloth of nettles.

"And slowly, slowly, she began to see the end of her long and laborious task."

"As her body grew rounder with new life dawning within it, the nettle thread was carded and spun. The many yards of cloth were woven. The shirts were carefully cut from the cloth and stitched by hand with a needle of iron (for iron is a sovereign cure against enchantment, particularly the evil kind.)"

"And sometimes swans were seen, flying in circles around the dawn lit tower."

"And at last, the young queen was brought to bed, and her long-awaited child was born. A son. A beautiful, perfect new son. Her heart was like to burst with joy, and her husband the king was likewise full of happiness at their new child."

"And the entire kingdom rejoiced."

"All save for the evil queen mother, of course."

"The evil queen was choked with spite and resentment. She resented the power that she had lost when her son the king had found love. Resented the joy that the king and maiden had found together. Resented how everyone around her also seemed to wish the interloper and her son only joy."

"Evil found a home in her heart. And she resolved to open her son's eyes to the enchantment that this girl had surely set upon him. To break the uncanny hold that she held upon him. To set the kingdom right again."

"No matter what it took to do so."

"The young queen continued to sew in her tower room, and to hold silent all the while as she did so. She brought the royal cradle to the tower room and cuddled her son the while she worked, but neither word, nor note, nor mother's coo would pass her lips, for to do so would doom her brothers to the curse forever."

"The evil queen took note of this unnatural behavior. It only served to confirm what she was sure of in her heart."

"And then, one day, while the young queen sewed a shirt and tickled her new born son beneath the chin, her mother-in-law visited her in her sun lit tower room, bearing a regal goblet filled with a liquid with a scent so wondrous that all who smelled it were sorely tempted by it."

"Daughter–in–law, I have brought this healing draught for thee and thee alone" smiled the evil queen mother. "It has a special gift to renew the strength and health of a woman who has given birth, for to bear a child is an arduous task indeed. When I gave birth to your husband the king, this rare and precious drink restored me fully, that I might be the best mother possible to him."

"The young queen was touched at the older woman's kindness. Smiling and gesturing her thanks, she took the goblet and drained it down."

"And collapsed to the floor, drugged and deep in slumber."

"A shadow crept softly across the queen mother's face, as she gazed at the fallen body of her daughter – in – law. She took a deep, shuddering breath.

And then she crossed to the cradle…."

Sixteen
Plots and Plagues

The Unseelie lord was feeling much better now. He had taken the first steps to set the swan folk against the people of the Seelie court, and he had told his retainers to sell the swan girl to the sorcerer who lived out in the bad lands. The sorcerer was always looking for subjects to work his magic on. His home was ringed around with such powerful wards that it was unlikely that anyone would be able to find her there.

The Unseelie lord thought. The Mantelfiederfolk were powerful adversaries indeed. Conflict between them and the despised Seelie warriors would leave both sides damaged and weakened, ripe to be overrun.

It was not enough though. The swan folk were strong in both arms and magic, but he wanted to tip the scales even more in their favor. The more damage they could do, the more vulnerable the Seelie would be.

Knowledge is power. He stood and crossed to the shelves looming over his oaken desk. Pulling down one book after another, he began to look for answers.

Hours later, he found one and began to laugh. Yes, that would do nicely.

He began to draw the circle, readying himself for a major casting. He had something special to send to the court of the Seelie.

Seventeen
The Story Continues

By now, Morgan was hunched up to the front of her chair with the quilt pulled tight around her, intent on the story that Sam was telling her.

He was a very good storyteller.

Sam paused for just a minute, and Morgan exploded.

"So, what happened next, Sam?" she demanded hungrily. "Did the evil queen do something evil to the young queen? Did she do something awful to her baby? (and how could she even think of doing such a thing? That's her grandson there.) Did the young queen survive? Did she finish the nettle shirts or not? Did she finish all of the nettle shirts? Did she save her brothers or were they cursed to remain in the form of swans forever? And what's with all of these evil older women running around in those days? Was it something in the water?"

"Give it up, Sam!" she insisted.

"Put a lid on it..." said Sam, gesturing for silence with one velvet paw. 'We're getting there, Morgan, we're getting there. Do you want to hear the story or not?"

Morgan clamped her lips shut and nodded vigorously.

"All right then" said Sam. "Here we go..."

"The evil queen mother had planned ahead for this night very carefully, very carefully indeed. She lifted the tiny baby from out of the cradle and took him from the room. When she returned to the room, she had a heavy earthen pitcher in her hands. The pitcher was full to the top with blood – the blood of a small animal that she had secretly slaughtered herself earlier in the day. She placed the pitcher carefully aside and went to her work."

"She crossed to the cradle and overturned it, scattering the bedding violently across the room. She threw other pieces of furniture around the tower room, creating a scene of violence and chaos. Taking the pitcher, she poured blood liberally over cradle and bedding, and splotched it on the floor surrounding the layette."

"Then, cautiously, she bent down over the sleeping form of her daughter–in–law and meticulously smeared some of the remaining blood on the young queen's hands and then her mouth."

"The queen mother stood back up and walked to the door, taking the golden goblet and the earthen pitcher with her. At the doorway, she stopped and looked back, contemplating the scene she had set. She paused and adjusted one piece of bedding, to perfect the effect."

"Perfect…"

"The evil queen smiled, and left the room."

"It was many hours later when the young queen began to stir, with a furious ache in her head and a funny taste in her mouth. Dizzily, she slowly rolled over and pulled herself to a sitting position."

"Her eyes gradually focused. She looked around her and found herself in a scene of horror."

"The room was in upheaval. Blood everywhere she looked. And where, oh where was her child?"

"Her vision swam."

"And an anguished shout came from the door way…"

"Turning, still dizzy, she saw her husband, the king standing in the door. His eyes were wide with horror and grew wider and wider still as he looked at her and the chaos around her."

"Where… is …. our…son?" he shouted at her. "Where…is…our … son? What … have…. you…done … to … him?"

"She wanted to answer him. She wanted to scream. It was only the practice and the discipline of her many years of silence that gave her the strength to hold silent."

"But the silence took its toll."

Exhausted with confusion, and horror, and fear for her child, and her husband's betrayal, and the effort of keeping her silence, lest a single word doomed her brothers to their curse, the young queen fainted away there on the floor in the midst of the pool of blood."

"They did not want to believe that such a horrid thing could happen. But the baby was gone, and the blood was everywhere, and the young queen did not say a word in her own defense, only cried and cried and cried soundlessly."

"And the king was dressed in mourning black, and all of his kingdom joined him in grieving for the young life lost to him."

"And the evil queen mother was oh so very, very kind and understanding throughout it all, saying that no doubt the young queen had gone through some terrible experiences in the swamp to make her lose her voice and harm her child in such a manner, and that it no doubt was not altogether her fault."

"And she only smiled when she knew no one was watching. But the smile that she smiled then was full of teeth, like a tiger."

"And the tower room that had been a delight to the young queen was now a chamber of horrors and a prison; for the slaughter of a royal heir is a most serious thing, and the young queen was to be tried for her crime and punished."

"And, as the time appointed for the trial grew closer, the young queen sat in her barren tower room and sewed – sewed furiously in order to complete the six nettle shirts before she came to judgment."

"The shirts must be finished, whether she survived her trial or not. Whether she lived or died, she couldn't leave her brothers trapped by the curse of her evil stepmother."

"She had had many hours of time to think in her prison. She had realized that the queen mother's cup had caused her to swoon, and that the evil queen herself must have caused her baby to vanish."

"Her only chance to exonerate herself was to speak at her trial- but to speak was to damn her brothers to her stepmother's curse."

"And, at last, at long last, the day came."

"They took the young queen unto the place of judgment, where her husband pronounced the ultimate sentence upon her with bright tears in his eyes. They brought her back to her tower room, to prepare her for her fate. They brought her from the tower to the cart, to carry her to her place of execution."

"And all the while, the young queen still held silent, sewing furiously as the tears flowed down her face."

"And at last she came to the place where she was to be burned to death at the stake, for the horror of the crime she stood accused of precluded her from a noble and merciful death by sword or axe at the hands of the royal executioner."

"She stepped down from the humble cart that had carried her, her slender arms filled top full of shirts of nettle cloth. She walked slowly and with quiet dignity to the stake, still sewing with strength and skill upon the shirts of nettles."

"She was firmly bound to the stake, needle still flying furiously as she worked at the final shirt, sewing a fine seam as they piled the wood to mound it up around her knees."

"And the people drew closer, in order to see the execution of the beautiful young queen; and not a single voice was raised in her defense, not even that of her husband the king, who stood and bore witness with tears flowing down his face and the evil queen mother close at his elbow, whispering into his ear."

"And the headsman lit the torch and touched the burning brand to the mass of wood piled high around her. And still she sewed onwards as the first log smoldered and then burst into leaping flames."

"And then, at once, everything changed."

Eighteen
Leaving a Clue

They had been on the move for a long time now. Bound, gagged and blindfolded, and slung over the back of a horse, the swan princess was turned around and unsure of where she was, but there were still certain indicators that she could detect if she was just alert and clever enough to pay attention.

The air was cool and damp, with a slight smell of moisture. The ride itself was rough, with her body jouncing up and down against the withers of the horse, even with the steeds moving at a walk. The horses' hooves were muffled and quiet. They must be on soft ground then, a path as opposed to a paved road, and one old or out of repair, judging by the footing for the animals. The ride was continuous- no branches to hold or cut back, so they were moving through relatively open terrain. She could hear the sound the horses' hooves made echoing back from tall features around her. Isolated trees then, or maybe even buildings, although probably not inhabited ones, since her captors made no efforts to conceal themselves and there were not any sounds of life to be heard other than that of the Unseelie party that bore her on to an unknown destination.

Her swan guards had been cut down. Though she had heard that one of them might have escaped and had not heard that he had been caught again, she had to assume that there was no help coming from that quarter.

She was alone, cut off, and, as far as she knew, not a soul who had a care for her knew where she was or even that she was still alive. While magick could be of help in such circumstances,/ and swan magick was puissant and powerful, from what she had heard her captors had magick of their own which might be proof against her mother's

57

powers. Her mother's magick might not be able to find her, and she had no magick of her own that would serve her in her current situation. She was alone here. Totally on her own. In the hands of her enemies.

Her spirit quailed for a single moment, and then her jaw tensed. She would not, could not be afraid, even in a situation like this one. She was not some weak and timid little mouse–like victim. She was a swan princess of the Mantelfiederfolk, a proud and noble race of warrior folk- a people who would not be beaten by trials such as this.

She was a warrior. While things might seem hopeless and she might seem helpless right now, it was her duty to do everything in her power to take from her captors any advantage that she could possibly manage. She did not know if any of her people would find where she had been taken, but she could at least try to leave evidence of her passing if one did.

Her wrists were bound together tightly behind her with narrow strips of leather. The leather bit into her skin and her fingers were gradually going numb. She wiggled them as best she could to keep what function and feeling she could within them.

Stretching, twisting, pulling, she gradually shifted her hands within her bonds until, at last, she could get the tips of two fingers on the clasp of her bracelet.

She tugged at it. Scraped her finger tips repeatedly across the metal closure. Twisted her bracelet between her wrists and against the rope until at last she felt the clasp give way and the bracelet sag against her skin.

And then it was wriggle, twist, and stretch again until at last she could work the bracelet free of the ropes that bound her.

The bracelet dropped softly and quietly into her palm. She breathed deeply for a moment, and then tossed it outwards with a subtle movement, hoping that the metal arching through the air would not shine in a stray sun beam and alert her captors. Hoping that tossing it outwards might make the bracelet fly and keep the jewel from being trodden into the mud beneath the horses' hooves.

The bracelet flew- and her prayers flew after it.

And the horses moved on into the unknown.

She waited then- waited for some outcry, some sign that her actions had been noted and would now be put at naught –

But her jailors did not seem to have even noticed.

A proud fire burned in her heart for a moment. She was not as helpless as they believed her to be. She was alone now. But her people would surely find her.

Borne off into the unknown, the swan princess began in earnest to plan her next strike against the forces that held her.

And her bracelet lay on the ground behind her, glistening.

Waiting.

Nineteen
Plague

No one had noticed at first when it started. A little tickle of the throat here. A minor cough there. A brief feeling of unsteadiness- of warmth, or weakness, or dizziness.

But all too soon, it was raging through the Seelie court, and more of the members of the court had contracted it than had not.

Inhabitants of the court felt shaky. Felt achy. Lost their appetites. Lost their strength. Took to their beds in droves.

The healers were quickly overwhelmed. Many of them came down with the unknown illness themselves. The guard rosters were short of healthy personnel, and working double shifts and short staffed was likely to put the remainder of the defenders out of commission in short order. The other workers of the court fell sick one by one, and the gaps in the running of the community became more and more evident.

The business of the Seelie court came to a grinding halt.

They called it the autumn bane, and it had seized the Seelie court by the throat while they were unawares.

In the highest tower, the seneschal sat by the young king's bedside, feeding him sips of soup and juice, and wiping his brow with a cool cloth in an attempt to bring down the raging fever. His own head swam, but he knew that his responsibility to the kingdom began with the well-being of its ruler.

He rang the bell at the bed side, and, after a long pause, an exhausted looking young guard opened the door to the bed chamber, entered, and looked at him expectantly.

"We have done as best we can in the face of this plague" said the seneschal "but it seems that what we can currently do is not enough to stem the tide. Go to my office and consult the references in the tall brown file on the right side of my desk. Those are our outside alliances – the people we may reasonably call on for help in our current crisis, and that we may trust during times of vulnerability. Send word to any outside healers, who may be able to turn this wave of sickness around; to any warriors who can step in to guard our borders, and to any workers who would be willing and able to staff our court until our own people have at last recovered."

"Yes, my lord" said the guard, and turned to go.

"…And, Terrance" said the seneschal.

The guard turned back to face him.

"Hurry…" said the seneschal, weakly.

Twenty
Happily Ever After..?

The blond stranger moaned a bit in his sleep. Morgan put her quilt aside and stood up from her chair, crossing the room to check once more on their unexpected visitor. He lay sleeping, curled around his wounds, motionless on the floor. His face was pale and his breathing uneasy, but his pulse was good and he seemed to be stable.

She tucked the blankets around him, shifting a pillow to block a draft. He shifted uneasily before settling once more firmly into slumber.

Morgan returned quietly to her chair, tucked the quilt around her once more, and returned her attention to Sam's story.

"With a trumpeting blast of sound, six massive winged figures dropped down from the heavens." said Sam. "Six swans broke into sight, six enormous swans of unearthly size and power landing in the town square. The crowd surrounding the briskly burning execution fire took an involuntary step backwards and then another in the face of so much fierceness."

"The flock of swans trumpeted loudly as one and dashed their bodies ferociously at the people there assembled, striking with wings like battering rams at royal and executioner and commoner alike. They flew into peoples' faces, confusing them with a flurry of feathers, and battering and stunning them with vicious blows from their wings. They landed on the ground and waddled forwards in a manner that was in somehow not comical, but rather intimidating and frightening. They hissed like king cobras, striking out with their beaks and biting at what-so- ever portion of the person was available to them. They moved with military precision, combined with raw power and fearlessness."

"The people who, but a moment ago, had been so eager to see their young queen burned alive, were now even more eager to leave the situation altogether. The onlookers at the front of the crowd turned and tried to run away, but the people further back in the back rows, still dumbstruck by the incursion of the swans, did not make way for them, resulting in major deadlock in the crowd. People ran to and fro, shrieking. Folks ran into each other, knocking each other down and stepping on each other. Sparks flew up from the still burning fire and set a dozen small blazes in the clearing around them, giving far better light for all to see the chaos and confusion."

"There were swans flying through the air. There were swans waddling ferociously along the ground. There were wings and beaks and trumpeting confronting you no matter in what direction you turned."

"And there was one particular swan on a mission."

Throughout the chaos, the young king stood frozen in impotency and despair, with the evil queen mother muttering words that no one else could hear constantly and insistently into his ear. He neither moved nor acted nor showed any reaction at all to the frenetic scene before him, neither fear, or sorrow or resolution."

"He continued frozen, even when the largest swan broke out of the crowd and came lunging forwards at him and the evil queen mother."

"Frozen he was – and for a moment, the queen mother froze as well. And the largest swan did too."

"Time passed – like amber honey dripping slowly from a spoon."

"And then the largest swan lunged and seized the evil queen mother firmly by the nose."

"There was certainly no more evil whispering then! There was screaming and crying and threatening and pleading though."

"And the largest swan set his feet and put his back into it and hauled upon that queenly (although evil) nose, until all of the rest of the queen mother had no other possible choice than to come along with it or to lose face altogether."

"And, as the queen mother was vigorously drawn away from him, a change came over the king's face – an expression as of one awakening from out of a dark dream. And looking up and seeing his lady wife there amongst the flames, the look of awareness was replaced with one of total horror; and the king leapt towards his wife, the young queen."

"As the largest of the swans had had a special mission and now continued to execute feats of ballroom dancing with the queen mother held firmly by her aristocratic nose, so the smallest of the swans also had a special mission of his own. As his fellow swans drove the townspeople back from the pyre and kept them concerned with other more important things, he landed in the center of the fracas and waddled briskly towards the young queen standing bound amongst the flames. Moving effectively and efficiently, he beat back with his wings the flames that lapped at the feet of the young queen, and then smothered the fire with the feathers of his breast. And he took neither burn nor blemish (for he was **that** kind of swan.)"

"Now, as the king leapt forwards through the confusion towards the execution fire, he was greeted eye to eye with the intelligent gaze of the smallest swan (for smallest was only a relative term, and, even lying down, the eyes of the smallest swan were directly on the level with those of the young king himself.)"

"The king froze again, the cries of the queen mother echoing in his ears. He was suddenly painfully aware of the tremendous power of those white wings, the sharpness of that pointed beak, and the awareness in the eyes that gazed into his."

"The swan paused for one v–e–r–y long moment; and then nodded its head ever so slightly and withdrew a few scant inches only, that the king might go to the young queen."

"Cautiously, the king slid by the enormous bird, and stepped into the smoldering wood pile, where his lady wife was as yet furiously sewing upon a shirt. Passing behind her, he reached for the ropes binding her in place and undid the tightened knots, one by one."

"Can you forgive me, my love?" begged the young king.

"The young queen gave him a very hard stare indeed; and the king felt very small and ashamed."

"The ropes fell away, and the young queen stepped away from the stake, away from the king and out of the execution pyre. Sparks dropped from her smoldering clothes as she stepped down onto the ground. The swans ceased their trumpeting, and lunging, and chasing of people; and lined up in a circle in front of her, like children at story time awaiting milk and cookies."

"The people all stared slack-jawed and amazed at the uncanny sight, even the king still by the stake, and the evil queen, who had a bloody nose and a headache, and was beginning to wonder if she had been making terribly good life choices lately."

"One by one, the young queen took the six nettle shirts and threw them over the snowy heads of the six massive swans, loose full sleeves passing easily over the powerful wings. One by one, she pulled the shirt hems

66

downwards, like a caring mother gently tucking her beloved little son into his clothing for the day. And one by one, the six enchanted swans turned back into her six, no longer cursed, brothers again."

"There was a long pause while everyone stopped to think about all of this."

"And then the young queen turned and pointed an accusing finger fiercely at the evil queen mother."

"*YOUR MOTHER!*" she shrieked furiously, transfixing the king with a glance of iron. "*YOUR MOTHER!!! Do you know what your mother has done?*""

"The king, still frozen at the stake, suddenly felt like he was about five years old. He cleared his throat nervously."

"Well, evidently not." he said nervously. "Why don't you tell me now?"

"*YOUR MOTHER! YOUR MOTHER!*" she shrieked, stuttering due to the intensity of the months just passed. "*Your mother drugged me! She covered my room with blood and put it on my lips. She lied about me! She made it look like I'd done something horrible. She framed me for infanticide! She did something awful to our baby!*"

"*And she actually got you to believe her wicked, wicked lies! You actually believed her! You believed that I would harm our baby, the child that we both loved so deeply!*"

"The young queen strode forward, and the world was in her stride. She reached the queen mother and pointed her accusing finger directly at her tattered nose."

"*What have you done to my baby, you evil, evil, evil hag?*" shouted the enraged young queen, in a voice like thunder coming over the mountains."

"The queen mother recoiled from the furious girl, protectively clutching at her bloodied and mangled nose. She had evidently gone just a little bit overboard in this situation.

She would have to think a little more carefully about this sort of thing before taking such action in the future."

"My dear, dear daughter – in – law," she began somewhat hesitantly. "I'm afraid that there has been a tiny misunderstanding here…"

"A misunderstanding?!? A misunderstanding?!?" the young queen howled. *"What is wrong with you?!? Are you totally insane?!? You have framed me for the death of my infant son! You have just tried to have me executed by burning me alive at the stake! You have made my baby, the beautiful baby boy that I love so much (and your own grandson, by the way), vanish! What–have–you–done– with–my–baby?!?"* she screamed hysterically, grabbing the evil queen by the front of her ornate robe and shaking her vigorously for emphasis."

"The king cautiously started to move forwards, fearing that he might be about to observe an act of matri– in–law–cide at any moment here."

"My dear…" he started, querulously."

"The young queen turned and looked at him fiercely. The king abruptly decided that prudence was certainly the better part of valor and closed his mouth again tightly."

"The young queen turned her burning gaze back to the eyes of the evil queen, who was suddenly wishing furiously that she had made the choice to be elsewhere today. Anywhere. Anywhere without a crowd and swans and especially a daughter–in–law would do."

"Your baby?..." the evil queen mother said. "Your baby? My dear, there must be some mistake. I have nothing to do with what happened to your baby"

"As you well know … " she hissed, eyes narrowing."

"The young queen's eyes widened in shock. Surely her mother-in-law could not be trying even now to control the situation with her lies."

"I have not one thing to do with what—so-ever has become of my beautiful grandchild the prince," said the evil queen mother "and I weep with all of my heart for the fact that *who—so-ever has taken him* has obviously made away with him, and that we will never know what *horrible, painful fate has seized upon that innocent baby boy."* she said, staring meaningfully into her daughter–in–law's eyes.

The young queen gasped. She wrang her hands until there were deadly white. A crystal tear leaked out of her eye and trickled softly down her snowy cheek.

"It is a pity" said the evil queen mother more confidently now "that we shall never ever know what has become of that poor, defenseless, helpless child- unless some person who knows the truth of things is given sufficiently good reason to speak openly and give that information freely to us."

"And she gave the young queen a cruel and significant look."

"The young queen's heart broke within her. And then her anger flared again, like the flames that had leapt up to consume her at the stake. She drew back her dainty but powerful little fisted hand. The evil queen mother looked nervous and covered her nose again, her confidence suddenly lost to her again as quickly as it had come."

"But that is not true," came a voice from behind her."

"Everyone turned."

"It is not true that our nephew, the young prince, is forever lost to us until sometime that some black hearted villain chooses to break his <u>or her</u> peace in exchange for some ill-gotten reward" said the youngest swan brother, in a casual conversational tone. "We are his uncles, and we were always there with him, keeping watch in turn over our sister and her child."

"Always there" he said more emphatically, looking

directly at the queen mother."

"The color drained from her face, and she swallowed hard, once."

"We watched, oh honored Mother of the King, as your jealousy and your resentment of our sister grew and festered within you" he said calmly yet firmly."

"We watched you betray every principle of nobility that a royal personage should embody."

"We watched as you drugged our sister with a sleeping draught."

"We watched as you made a shambles of the tower nursery, and spattered it with blood."

"We watched as you took our nephew from his cradle."

"We watched as you accused our beloved sister by making weak excuses for her, always stumbling so "regretfully" over things that only seemed to point to her guilt."

"We watched you see that our sister was condemned to death by burning, and that her husband was too deep in thrall to your words and your whispering to care for or to save his unjustly condemned wife."

"And we watched as you gave our nephew, *your own sweet grandchild,* to your most trusted huntsman, bidding him to take the infant to the heart of the enchanted swamp where our sister was first found and to abandon him there, exposing him to the mercy of the elements and of all the fearsome creatures and enchanted mysteries that were to be found there."

"We followed that huntsman, as he set about his black and unholy deed, and when he came into the swamp, where there was no one there to help him in his wickedness, we flew at him, blinding him, beating him, taking the baby safely from him. Our nephew is now secure in the hands of those who wish us and him well, and your huntsman shall never be seen again in the ways of man."

"The queen mother shuddered, and swallowed hard again."

"So, what, oh so honored Mother of the King and Grandmother of the living Prince, should be the penalty for one who conspires at such deeply foul deeds and so many of them, all in the service of her own base vanity and hunger for power?" the youngest brother said sharply, his eyes piercing her to the core."

"er….er…" stuttered the evil queen mother. "There seems to have been some kind of misunderstanding…"

"There was a brief pause, while everyone tried their best to absorb the fact that the evil queen still thought that talking could make this all go away."

"No one could quite manage it, somehow."

"Enough, Mother!" roared the king, suddenly incensed. "There will be enough of your lies!"

"The queen mother squeaked in surprise. Of all things possible, she had certainly not been expecting her son to stand up to her."

"To the stake with her!' the king shouted. "Let she in turn receive the punishment that she had prepared for my blameless lady wife!" And, passing swiftly to the young queen, he looked at her inquiringly and held his arms slightly open."

"The young queen gave him another hard look. And then, seeing the sorrow and apology in his face, her face softened slightly and she gave a tiny nod."

"He wrapped his arms and his cloak around her and began to whisper gently in her ear."

"And the evil queen was dragged to the waiting stake, still wildly protesting that this must be some kind of dreadful mistake. And she was tied to the stake with leather cords, still struggling and protesting loudly. And the wood was set alight again, and the crackling flames leaped up, and she stopped protesting at about that point."

"And, after a while, she died. Because that is the way that they did things in those days."

"And the missing young prince was brought safely home from out of the swamps by some rather unusual folk (and he continued to have remarkable companions for all of the rest of his life), none the worse for his infant adventures. And his relieved parents, the king, and the young queen, and his six uncles, and all of their kingdom besides rejoiced and made merry at his blessedly safe return. And, if there were some hard looks and harder words and some terse discussions in the royal bower for quite some time thereafter, that would not be something that neither you or I would need to be privy to (thank heavens!)"

"But the king, and the young queen, and her six swan brothers, and the healthy young prince lived happily ever after."

Twenty-One
Summons

The palmist was sitting at the computer, typing furiously away at an article for a local metaphysical magazine. Her husband, the tarot reader, was in the kitchen, experimenting with preparing mushrooms in a savory sauce to top a perfectly prepared steak.

As she typed, he came into the office with a big spoon and a bigger grin on his hirsute face.

"Taste it." he said, holding the spoon to her lips. "What does it need? It needs something, but I can't quite put my finger on what."

The aroma was wonderful.

The palmist blew gently on the spoon, carefully sucked the mushroom sauce off of it, and tasted it thoughtfully.

"It's very good" she said finally. "I think if it were for me, I would like it just a tad sweeter, but you prefer more piquant flavors, and since it's for your steak…"

"Garlic!" he said. "That's it! That's what it's missing! That's what it needs – more garlic!"

"Well, doesn't everything?" she said, smiling fondly up at him and continuing to type briskly.

There was a light tapping at the window.

She looked at him. He looked at her.

"It's your turn" she said.

"Hey, my hands are full." he replied, brandishing the spoon.

She looked at him for a moment more.

"Well, o.k." she said finally, "but if something fell leaps through the window at <u>my</u> face once I draw back the curtains, you'll owe me a mushroom sauce for <u>my</u> steak."

She turned back to the window and drew the curtains aside. She cautiously peered out and her face softened. "Aaaww!" she said and pushed the window open.

A tiny grey tabby kitten with even tinier wings tumbled in at the window and into her lap as she neatly moved to catch him. He rolled around for a minute, snatching at his tail and getting his balance before he remembered himself, and pulled himself together into a miniature image of cat –tish dignity.

"M-ss-ge" lisped the kitten, sitting as upright and proper in her lap as his age permitted.

"Aaaww!" said the short, round woman again. "What was that, dear?"

The tarot reader leaned in closer to hear, an "aww" lurking on his kindly face as well.

The grey kitten settled itself even more officially and took the time to carefully enunciate.

"...M-ess-age..." said the kitten, very gravely. "Lissen up. De see-lie court be-set by horr-end-ous sickness. Most of court sev–ere-ly ill and bed bound. Plague beliefed to be of mag–ick-al or-i-gins. Call to all mystic healers to come n' help wid takin' care uv people, and findin' an' stoppin' whose makin' it happen. Plees help. Dis is all. End of m–ess-age..."

He held his small yet appreciable dignity for yet another moment, and then smiled at her and cuddled into her arms, purring-his duty done.

The palmist smiled at him, and then her face turned serious.

"You've done a great job" she said carefully, in respect to his tiny ego "but why isn't your mother bringing us this message, as she usually does?"

The kitten looked up at her with serious eyes.

"Big catz sick" he said. "All de big cats sick.

Ebrybuddy sick, sick, sick."

"Cept me." he added and curled up in her arms once more, hiding his nose beneath his paws.

Face suddenly somber, the palmist held the kitten close for just a moment before gently depositing him on the quilt in the rocking chair in the corner, amidst much feline complaining.

"Grab the healing kits," she said, looking at her husband. "I'll run upstairs and pack us each a bag. This looks like it's going to be a big one. The odds are good that we may be on–call for a while."

"I'm on it" he said briskly, already heading out of the room. "Just give me a minute to scrape this sauce into a container and pop it into the fridge, and I'll go load what we need in the car."

The kitten yowled querulously, begging to be picked up as the palmist moved about the room, popping key items into a carry-all. She dashed out of the room, returning shortly with a pair of well stocked backpacks and a canvas sack full of bits and pieces, arriving at the same time as the tarot reader, with a pair of big plastic cases of metaphysical healing supplies and a couple of sandwiches for the road.

"Ready?" said the tarot reader.

The palm reader grabbed a book off of the shelf. "Ready!" she said.

She turned back to the kitten that was still standing in the rocking chair and blinking about him furiously.

"We're going to the Seelie court, and you can't stay here without us. Would you have somewhere to be flying to, or would you like to go back to the court with us?"

The kitten looked at her with big wide eyes and thought about it for a moment.

"Wanna go wit yu two." he decided.

"We're honored" said the tarot reader, gently

picking him up. The winged kitten snuggled into his arms and began to bat playfully at trailing wisps of his beard.

The tarot reader took the winged kitten to the car and returned for the healing kits. The palmist made a last circuit of the house, turning off lights, closing and locking windows and doors before pausing at the front door with a troubled look on her face.

"Spirit of our hearth, please watch over our home while we are both away from it. I don't know how long we'll be gone, and I don't know what may happen while we're away but thank you for guarding our home."

She turned out the final light and left.

Twenty- Two
After the Happy Ending

"And that's the end of the story..." said Sam, kneading the pillows and adjusting himself slightly in order to find an even more comfortable spot on the overstuffed sofa.

"That was amazing!" said Morgan, the quilt still wrapped tight around her. "I've heard that story many times before in my life, but never told quite like that."

"But now I need to know" she added quickly "what does an old-fashioned traditional fairy tale like that have to do with our unexpected house guest?" she asked, looking towards the huddled bundle of blankets on the hallway floor. "And what does it have to do with why you were so upset when you saw who and what he was?"

"There's a really good reason for that, actually," said the cat. "As pretty much everyone truly knows, at least when they actually stop to think about it, whenever you say "The end" or "and they lived happily ever after..." at the end of a story, that's really not the end but rather the beginning." said Sam. "It's the beginning of a brand-new story."

Morgan stopped and thought about this, and then her face lit up with a big "a- ha".

"I get it" she said. "So, what's the new story that goes on from that point?"

Sam looked at her seriously for a moment. "Now, everybody thinks that the story ends there, right?"

"well it does...and it doesn't..."

"It does end there because the brothers Grimm chose to end it there because it gave them a fairly happy and moral ending, which is what they were looking for. But the real story, the true story itself went on."

"The swan princes were glad to regain their mortal

77

forms- that much was true. But, once they got past the excitement of having their curse finally lifted, they also found that they missed living the life of a swan. They missed the freedom. They missed the sweep of their strong white wings as they bore them skywards. They missed the ability to fly where ever they would and the broader, wider world they gained throughout their flying. They missed their fierceness. They missed their closeness as a wedge of warrior brothers."

"Most of all, they missed the glories of flight. They missed the ability to make the heavens their own."

"They were certainly glad to be men once more. And yet… yet… still they hungered to be swans again."

She thought about that.

"I can see that, I think" nodded Morgan, on reflection. "Being swans would have limited them severely, but at the same time, it would have opened wide new horizons to them they never would have experienced if they'd never been swans."

"You've got it." nodded Sam, pleased. "It's the classic dichotomy – do you want roots or do you want wings?"

"The answer was that they wanted both." he said. "So, they set out on their own personal quest to find how this could be accomplished."

"And as the six brothers–in–law of a very affluent king (who was feeling rather guilty about the poor way he had treated their sister during a marital crisis), they had more than ample resources to look for the answer."

"They inquired of many wise and learned people. They traveled far and wide. They did prolonged research in the volumes of many deeply hidden libraries. They studied with various mystical masters. They set a reward for any information leading to the information that they sought."

"And, in time, their diligence was rewarded."

"They finally found a way to achieve their dream. Not one that would bind them in the body of a swan at all times. Not one that would permit them to assume the body of a swan with nothing but the application of their own wills. But one that enabled them to put on and take off their swan form as easily as someone donning a cloak."

"Indeed, the secret involved a cloak – a magickal cloak made out of swan feathers. When you put it around yourself, you became a swan. When you took it off, you were a man once more."

"This was a great magick, and one that would not work for just anyone who tried it. It worked for the six swan brothers because, while the curse had been laid to rest by the courage and hard work of their sister, the shape of the swan still sparkled in their blood and called to them in their dreams. They knew what it was to walk in the shape of a swan, and to fly in it. The knowing of that enchanted shape, combined with the cloak of feathers could allow them to become something far more magickal than a man."

"Now, it is educational and instructional and useful to know that the lands in which these stories happened were of the wild lands- the lands full of little pocket kingdoms that became the country that we know as Germany much later in the scheme of things. And so it was that, when at last they created this wonderful and magickal cloak of feathers, they gave it a German name."

"This very special magickal cloak was called a "mantelfieder", drawing from the German word "mantel" meaning "cloak or coat", and the German word "fieder", meaning "feather". And, in honor of this wild magick, the six swan brothers began to refer to themselves as the Mantelfiederfolk (or "Fiederfolk" for short, if you prefer), meaning "the people of the feather cloaks".

"Having found their magick at last, they flew. They flew to the south, to deserts unending and traveling bands of horsemen in tents. They flew to the north, where the snow lay always on the ground and the great white bears were kings in their own right. They flew to the east, to a world of islands and dragons and enchanted fish. They flew to the west, to lands of bards and heroes and magick bound in words."

"The world was theirs. And they flew to it all."

"And their sister could not fly. But she sat and looked out of her tower window for them to return, before turning with a smile to play with her sturdy young son."

"And, in time, the six brothers all found brides. Their wives could not work the magick of the mantelfieder. They could not fly, since they had never walked the earth as swans so some of the brothers spent more time as men, at home with the women that they loved and some of the brothers continued to fly, spending their time with their families when they could."

"Their wives could not fly, cloak of feathers or no, but, when their children were born, they found that they all could. The magick of taking the shape of the swan, the magick needed to meld with the mantelfieder, the cloak of feathers, was living in their blood, and their blood ran all too true in their children's veins."

"Their children could fly and fly they certainly did."

Twenty-Three
Sold to a Sorcerer

Ariella had fought back hard against her attackers whenever she had the chance. She had marked them repeatedly with nails and teeth, and so they tied her hands behind her, tightly enough that her fingers were tingling as the circulation was gradually cut off. They had secured her legs together at the ankles as well. She was still blindfolded and gagged, unable to see where she was going or call for help if there was a chance of it. They had tossed her up on a horse in front of an unseen captor. He held her firmly in place with one muscular arm wrapped tightly around her while he carefully guided his horse with the other one.

She could feel the massive body of the horse moving beneath her and the body of her captor pressed uncomfortably close to hers, shifting with the movement of his mount. She could hear the sounds of the forest and of many other horses surrounding them as the Unseelie elven train rode through the forest in the darkness. She could feel the wind and the sense of riding up and down over uneven terrain, but she could not see where they were going or what was at the final end of their journey. She only knew that they seemed to ride for a very long time.

If she belonged to a lesser people, she might have been afraid, but the Mantelfiederfolk were a brave and strong people, a barbarian warrior race. They did not experience fear. Never.

They rode for what seemed a very long time and Ariella had no idea where they were going. She did her best to collect such clues as she could in her blinded and captive position, but there was only so much she could do.

At last, she could hear the sound of horses slowing and the elven train drew to a stop. She still could not see where she was, but there was a change in the light against her blindfold that implied that they had come to a place where there were torches or lanterns.

The horse she was seated on stopped, and unexpectedly and without ceremony, she was dumped from high on the back of the horse to the ground far below. Her breath burst forcibly from her with the impact and she did her best not to cry out from the pain of the fall. She was lying on her face on the ground, lying on sticks and on rocks and on uneven earth.

"A place inhabited" she thought hard, doing her best to focus her mind "but rustic- not well developed and in the forest hidden. If escape I can, probably no place close where help I can find. For a distance, I will have to run."

As she lay on her face in the dirt, she heard footsteps approaching her, crunching on the fallen twigs, and the light became brighter through the blindfold.

Without warning, a sinewy hand grasped her chin firmly, pulling her up into a seated position. Another hand pushed back the blindfold, revealing her face more fully in the lantern light. Ariella blinked repeatedly, half blinded by the light after being in darkness so long.

The hand held her chin firmly, not permitting any movement of face or of body as she crouched on the ground. It tipped her head back so that the person holding her face could see it more clearly in the half light.

"My…" an unfamiliar voice said slowly "What do we have here? Could it be? Why, yes. Yes- your master spoke truly. It is not often that a swan maiden comes onto the market, but here she is indeed. She will do nicely for my purposes."

Held immobile, Ariella felt her heart drop within her. She had heard fear described by other folks, but, since she was Mantelfiederfolk, what she was feeling now (the sweating of her brow, the roiling of her stomach, the slight trembling of her hands) could have nothing to do with fear-nothing at all.

Thank goodness.

The half seen other hand dropped lower, pulling back the cloak in the lantern light and revealing the swan maiden until now hidden underneath it.

"And she's young, too," said the unpleasant voice "and looks strong and healthy. All the better for what I have planned."

Ariella bit her lip and tried her best not to reveal any weakness her captor could use against her

"Yes, she will be fine" the unpleasant voice continued in a satisfied tone "a shining gem and a splendid addition to my collection. Thank your master for offering her first to me. Take her inside, boys."

Ariella then heard the clink of coins changing hands. Many coins.

Twenty-Four
Why a Swan Knight Means Trouble

By now, hours had passed, it was almost dawn and the first little sounds of birds chirping cheerfully were heralding the sun and preventing anyone else in the neighborhood from getting any more sleep. The first cautious light was peeping in through tightly pulled curtains, and the possibility that they would survive the night was almost certain.

Of course, today was another day.

"Well, that's certainly a great story," said Morgan, "but I'm still not getting exactly how that connects up to our current situation here. More words please."

"Well, the swan brothers had many children. And those children could take the feather cloak, the mantelfieder and the shape of a swan with it." said Sam.

"Yes…" said Morgan.

"And those children also had children. And those children could also take the mantelfieder and the shape of a swan." Sam said.

"And…" said Morgan.

"And those children had children. And those children could take the mantelfieder and the shape of a swan as well." added Sam.

"So…" said Morgan.

"And so on, and so on, and so on, throughout the years and the generations, and right up to the present day." said the golden cat.

There was a long pause

"No!" gasped Morgan, suddenly understanding. "You're not saying…"

"I am indeed," said Sam. "That hunk of cuts and bruises under your grandmother's quilt on the foyer floor is an actual, gen–u–ine swan knight. Patent pending."

Morgan wheeled about and stared in new fascination at her unexpected guest for a moment. She got up and walked over to their visitor, circling him slowly and looking at him from all sides.

She turned back to Sam, scowling.

"He doesn't actually look very "swan–ish" she said, in a disappointed fashion. "Not a trace of a feather showing anywhere. With all that skin he's showing, I think I would have seen them if they were there."

"Look, Morgan." said Sam bluntly. "He's not some half–man / half–swan mutant. He's not a swan *all* the time, girl. But he's definitely a swan knight. And that means trouble for us."

"Trouble for us?" said Morgan. "Why would that be trouble?"

"Well, there are several possible reasons to think about," said her feline companion from his seat on the sofa.

"First and foremost, even non-magical swans are very dangerous animals. People think of them as beautiful, peaceful birds, gliding serenely on the still surface of a peaceful crystal pool or on the front of formal wedding invitations, but a pissed off swan can do some major damage. Have you ever seen a swan attack? Yes? Then you know how fierce and war-like a swan can be."

"And this is a man who is sometimes a swan and sometimes a warrior, and who is raised from birth to be absolutely deadly in either form. And when he wakes up, he's going to be hurting badly and just may not remember who pulled him in off the porch, bound his wounds and concealed him from the boogey man. He may only remember pain and danger and cut loose with every single martial skill in his repertoire."

"That's only problem number one." said Sam.

An alarmed look ran quickly across Morgan's face. "Only problem one?" she thought in dismay.

"Second," continued the cat "the Mantelfiederfolk are, by their very nature, an extremely close knit and insular community. Doing your best to keep your supernatural powers and uncanny nature secret from the rest of the world can do that to you. And, like all close and secret communities, the Fiederfolk try very hard to distance themselves from the attention of the regular world."

"And here he is, his people's existance revealed; and the only things that put them at risk of having their secrets out in the open are the lives of one woman and her very attractive and intelligent talking cat. That's problem number two." said Sam.

"Third, the reason this handsome blond disaster came knocking at your door and messed up your floor is that something or ***things*** have rolled over the top of him, giving him all of those cuts, bruises, and wounds and sending him running for his life. Him – <u>a swan knight</u> – one of the more dangerous creatures in the worlds unseen – knocked for a loop and brought to within an inch of his life. Think about that for a moment." said the cat.

Morgan thought. The thoughts were not happy ones.

"Furthermore, if I heard him correctly (and I'm sure I did), he was not just a lone swan knight. Oh, no. He was riding as part of a full wedge of swan knights – a formal military patrol. And, from what he said, the wedge was guarding a swan princess, and only the absolute best of their most deadly warriors are assigned to important tasks such as that. So, we've got something that can take out an entire wedge of the best and most martial of the swan knights, steal a swan princess and still have enough savagery to hunt the lone survivor down?"

Sam looked at Morgan. Morgan looked at Sam.

"I see exactly what you mean," said Morgan. "Definitely trouble."

They both turned and looked at the sleeping swan knight, only to find his blue eyes open and watching them carefully.

They both froze.

"Stay calm." muttered Sam out of the corner of his furry mouth. "Stay calm. Don't alarm the nice swan knight."

"You know, ears ve svan knights are having!" the blond warrior shouted angrily. "Vat you say, I can hear."

He lunged upright and then his wounds caught him. He collapsed again, curling up into a ball with a hint of an echo of a whimper.

Morgan was across the room in a shot, and on her knees beside the battered man. She reached out gently but firmly, checking his major wounds to see if he had done himself any additional damage.

"Voman, off of me get!" the blond warrior hissed between gritted teeth. "Such pampering, a svan knight does not need."

"Swan knight or not," said Morgan firmly. "we pulled you in here off the porch last night in seriously bad shape with a number of major wounds, and I'll be darned if I'm going to patch you up and hide you from your enemies, only to have you die of drama and excessive movement. Lie still, you, while I check your wounds."

Grumbling but not yet ready for brisk movement, the swan knight settled down and co-operated.

Checking first chest, and then head, and, one by one, other wounds of lesser urgency and concern, Morgan was surprised to find that the blond warrior had healed far more quickly than she would have thought possible. Wounds that should have needed stitches and weeks of hospitalization, if he'd had survived at all, had become ugly scabs that seemed several weeks old, while lesser wounds had reached the ancient scar tissue stage. Her patient had healed at a rate that seemed impossible.

"But, what do I really know about how fast a swan heals, let alone a swan knight?" thought Morgan. She checked his pulse, and his forehead for fever as well, just to be on the safe side.

"Well, you do seem to be in much better shape now than I thought you'd be when you collapsed on my porch," she said to her patient "but I'd still take it easy on moving. We don't want you to start bleeding again."

The swan knight took a deep breath, gritted his teeth and sat up again, more slowly this time, pushing her aside gently but emphatically.

"Time, I do not have." he said somberly. "No time at all. Out there, a savage Death there is- a Death that our princess has taken, my companions killed and myself almost ended."

"As your furry friend has said" the swan knight added, nodding towards Sam "a Death that vith such ease a vedge of svan knights can destroy, is a Death vith vich to reckon."

"My people must be varned. That her daughter vas taken, my chieftainess must know. And, if necessary, the Mantelfiederfolk must for var prepare. As the only svan knight alive to varn my people, my duty it is."

He looked in Morgan's eyes, and saw something there that stopped him for a moment. His face softened, and then he spoke more slowly

"My lady, your concern I do appreciate, but time I

have not. Not to fear - ve svan knights quickly heal. My best, I must do- upon my healing, the Fiederfolk cannot vait."

He started to pull himself slowly into a kneeling position, then hissed sharply between his teeth, as bone grated upon bone deep within his chest. Morgan lunged forwards to support him and was met with the glare of a man who was going to do this for himself. She froze, unsure what she should do next.

Suddenly, Sam was there, fuzzy face poking cheerfully and inquisitively in between them.

"I don't think we've been introduced" he said. "I'm Sam and this is Morgan. And you are?"

The swan knight hesitated. "Vell, a little tricky, that is," he began slowly. "Amongst my people, a true name power has."

He stopped and looked at them, thinking things over.

"But, under these circumstances, Claud you may call me." he said at last.

He clambered heavily to his feet, and stood there in the foyer, swaying slightly. He tried his weight on the left leg, and grimaced at the results.

"So, my veapons vere they are?" said the big, blond Fiederfolk warrior.

Morgan looked at him and was suddenly irritated. Her jaw tensed, and her eyes narrowed.

"That's not happening now." she said, angrily. "You can barely stand on your own two feet. You're not going to be able to even make it to the door, and you're surely not going to be able to reach your own people in time, if they're anywhere further than the end of the block. Not to mention that you're definitely not going to be able to run the gamut of whatever dangers are out there waiting for you. You can barely walk, so how do you think you're going to make a run for it?"

The big man made a pained face as one leg gave way beneath him. He turned to look at her, considering.

"Fraulein, a point you are having, but matter it does not." he said. "Death, the land is stalking, the princess gone, and, against that, the life of a single svan as nothing is. Vhat vould you have me do? I must to my people go."

"What I'm saying is that you won't being going anywhere alone in your condition." she said firmly. "We'll both be going with you and seeing you safely back to your own people."

"What?!" said Sam behind her.

He wasn't the only one surprised and dismayed. "Vhat?! Nein!" the swan knight shouted. "Nein! For folks such as your cat and you, this kind of adventure is not! For varriors, this vork is, and varriors clearly you are not!"

She gave the angry swan knight a hard look then. She had a glare like a blowtorch.

He withered in the heat of her regard and looked abashed. "Your pardon, begging." he said.

Sam cleared his throat, and the two of them turned to look at him

"You may be a warrior" he said conversationally to the swan knight, "but let me tell you, this is one fight that you're definitely not going to win. Trust me on this, dude. Take a clue from someone who lives with her. Just go with the inevitable here- it'll save you a lot of aggravation."

Morgan turned and glared at him as well. Sam suddenly became very interested in his personal grooming.

Morgan turned back and glared at the blond Feiderfolk once more.

"You may be the most powerful warrior in the history of history, but on this day, you are going to listen to me. You're healing fast, but it's not fast enough. You're going to need us if you're going to reach your people, and you need to reach your people so you need us. We're going with you and That is That!"

The Feiderfolk blinked rapidly several times. He turned and looked down at the cat. The cat looked up at the Feiderfolk.

"Alvays like dis, she is?" asked the blond barbarian.

"Pretty much." said Sam. "Save yourself some time and capitulate now."

"Hey!" snapped Morgan. "Standing right here, guys! I have ears, too, you know."

Knight and feline turned to face her.

"Vat do you think?" muttered Claud out of the corner of his mouth.

"I'd say we do what she says to do." said Sam. "Save time, avoid arguments, and accept the inevitable."

"Vomen like this, before I have seen," muttered the swan knight "and, in resistance, no point there is. Vin ve vill not."

"Standing right here." repeated Morgan.

Two sets of eyes snapped instantly front and center.

"We're with you." said Sam.

"Yah." agreed Claud. "If you vish, vith me you may go."

Morgan blinked for a minute, startled for a moment by the sudden collapse of all opposition.

"Well, all righty, then" she said finally. "Let me find my car keys."

Twenty-Five
The Door is Damaged and the Gate is Marked

She picked up her keys, and then stopped to think for a moment. Reaching into the closet, she pulled out her bigger purse, and her most comfortable running shoes. She dropped the keys in the purse, and then sat down to change her shoes.

Because, you never know- and she remembered what things had been like last fall.

Sam was standing on the porch, looking closely at the front door, when Morgan emerged from the house. "Well, that's impressive" he said. "I think that we're gonna have to forfeit our rental deposit."

Morgan turned and looked at the door and gasped. Enormous scratches ran from the top to the bottom of the door, traversing its length with one massive stroke after another, and marking up the frame as well. Wordlessly, she stepped forwards and fitted one finger into a scratch. Her finger disappeared deep within the gouged-out space with plenty of room to spare.

"Wow." said Morgan, her eyes wide.

"Yes–sir–ee bob, those were some big paws that came a-knocking on our door last night. At least we kept our door, unlike the last time." said Sam complacently. "That guy who set up the wards for us? We need to send him a fruit basket or something."

Out of the corner of her eye, Morgan caught sight of something glistening against the front gate post.

"Just a minute," she said, and moved down the steps and to the gate in order to look more closely.

There was something written there on the fence post. There was something written there- she would swear to it, but every time she almost had it visually nailed down, it would slide away from under her gaze again. More extreme measures were evidently called for.

Not so long ago, when Morgan had first learned of the lands that lay between and set out on a wonderful, terrible journey through lands both mystical and mundane, she'd been gifted with a small container of the ointment of seeing, a rare and precious preparation that permitted the user to see all which was hidden, especially by magick. Being in dire straits at the time, not knowing how long an application would last, and not wanting to go around seeing mystical things that no one else could see all the time, Morgan had chosen to apply the ointment to only one eye.

It turned out that this process had included an excessive amount of tearing up, burning sensations, vigorous cursing, and dancing furiously around the library ladies room; but when her eye at last cleared, she could see the unseen, the hidden mysteries, and, by opening and closing one eye at a time, she could distinguish the unseen from the mundane world around her. This was very helpful to her when driving, shopping, and surfing the Internet.

And the power granted by the ointment had persisted up to this day.

Morgan closed her everyday eye now and looked at the fence post with the eye of seeing alone. There, on the fence post, she saw a mark, a mark she had not been able to see before.

"Sam" she said, pulling a small pad of paper and a pen from her purse and drawing a copy of what she saw, "what does this symbol mean?"

Sam wandered over casually and looked down at the paper. His tail stiffened. "Where did you see this, Morgan?" he asked.

"Right here" she said. "Here on the front gate post. I could hardly catch it at all until I used the "special" eye on it. What does it mean?"

Sam frowned as he inspected the gate post more closely, scowling and squinting as he concentrated. After a moment, he turned back to the paper again, finding it easier to analyze than the shimmering in–and–out marks on the gate itself. He turned back to stare at the gate post again, and then back to the paper once more.

"It's an elven sanctuary marking" he said finally. "It's the equivalent of the marks that hobos used to leave during the Great Depression outside of houses with kind and generous people. It says that our house is a haven for any being in trouble."

"Damn it!" Sam swore. "They've turned us into a general safe house, without even asking us first!"

Morgan shrugged.

"Well, that would explain some of the weird calls I've been getting lately. Knocks on the door with no one there. Doors and windows coming open. Phone calls with no one at the other end."

"We've gotta get that friend of yours to tweak those wards so they not only keep out evil, but also keep out all non-residents who do not have our express permission to enter." said Sam, still studying the gate post morosely. "I don't mind helping out, but I'd like to choose when I help someone and know if we have guests that may be drawing trouble after them."

"Sounds like a good thought" agreed Morgan. "I'd like to choose whether I play hostess myself."

"Just a minute, Morgan" said Sam. "I'll be right back."

He dashed back in through the damaged front door just as the Fiederfolk warrior stepped out of the house, settling hand axes in hip scabbards. The blond barbarian turned and frowned at the great scratches covering the door and the door frame.

"Ah dark hunds." he said. "A bad case of the dark hunds, you have got. A good thing, that is not."

Morgan's jaw dropped. She goggled at him.

"You know what made these marks?" she said.

"Oh, yah, sure." Claud said in a matter of fact manner. "All of the time, the dark hunds ve see. Very, nasty rascals, they are − into our trash always getting, and the warriors attacking, and the maidens menacing, and other naughty stuff like that there. A locking top on your trash can, you are going to have to put or rid of them, you vill never get."

In another minute, Sam re-emerged from the house, carrying something carefully wrapped in a napkin in his mouth. He crossed to Morgan's purse, and carefully deposited the napkin in it, while Morgan was still looking at the gate post.

"As long as we're at it, do you know anything at all about this mark here on the gate post?" Morgan called to Claud.

"Oh, jah, jah" he said. "lots of them marks and lots of other marks like them all the time too ve see. And, ven I vas running and running and thought that out of run in me I had run, there it vas, to a safe haven me velcoming."

"And here I am" he said, beaming. "Safe."

"Right." said Sam, slowly.

"Hey," the cat said, changing the subject, abruptly "aren't you going to attract an awful lot of attention walking around dressed like that? After all, most folks these days don't dress like extras from a sword and sandal fantasy movie."

Claud looked down rather confusedly at his loin cloth and collection of various pieces of armor and leather straps. His brow wrinkled when he thought about this for a moment, and then, he shrugged philosophically.

"No problem here, mein liddle friend!" he said cheerfully. "One of the powers of the Fiederfolk, is, in the vaking vorld, totally unnoticed to pass if ve should so choose."

Sam and Morgan looked at the 6 foot plus blond barbarian, dressed in an amount of metal and leather totally inadequate to cover his frame.

"Ri-ght..." Sam said again. "Let's get you in the car pretty quickly, shall we?"

Twenty-Six
Lair of the Sorcerer

Rough hands grasped Ariella, pulling her off of the ground and throwing her over a burly shoulder. She was carried away like luggage, helpless and unable to move.

She was carried into a tunnel and then down a long hallway, passing many doors on both sides. Her captor came at last into a larger open area, and roughly dumped her down on the stone floor.

"Here she is" said her bearer. "And I hope that you enjoy having her."

"Oh, I will. I certainly will." said the other voice, smooth, oily, and filled with a not so subtle menace. "The little swan princess and I have a lot of things to talk about."

"Well, have a nice *talk* then…" said the Unseelie warrior who had brought her here.

She could feel someone behind her approaching her. Could feel someone standing over her body and looking closely at her as she lay on the floor, helpless.

Ariella bit her lip and held her silence, trying her best not to scream out loud.

Twenty-Seven
Ambush

They had set off in Morgan's car on the way to the current encampment of the Mantelfiederfolk. Claud was sitting up front giving directions and Sam was sulking in the back, not in his usual designated position of honor. They'd made significant progress towards the edge of town, when suddenly they found themselves in a major traffic jam. A large truck was backing up into the street and blocking both lanes of traffic. They came to a total stop, tightly boxed in by other vehicles packed around them.

As they were sitting there, waiting for traffic to move, Morgan felt a prickling along her spine. Suddenly she felt uneasy.

Sitting at a complete halt, she was free to close her regular eye and see things only through the eye of seeing. The elven glamour cleared and she saw this was a trap- a trap set especially for them, or at least for their swan knight traveling companion.

There was a deep breath from the back seat.

Many of the more deadly parts of enchantment only roam the world at night. Morgan had hoped that traveling by daylight, they might avoid the worst of these.

In this case, evidently not.

With the illusions dissolved, she saw the truck athwart both lanes of the street was really a barricade of tangled wood and enchanted thorn. Some of the cars and trucks around them were actually rocks and bramble thickets, reaching out with spiny limbs or stony claws. The surrounding buildings were a narrow pass, with towering walls looming so high that they partially blocked the sun, leaving them sitting in shadow.

And the people.

Some were just ordinary people sitting in ordinary cars; singing along with the radio, thinking about what they needed to pick up from the market for supper, or gritting their teeth at the unexpected delay.

But not all of them.

Amidst the unaware everyday people were figures carved out of nightmares. Unseelie warriors, clad in metal, pain and shadow. Lesser evils, skittering through the crowded street, tittering hysterically. Black and fearsome hounds, stalking from car to car to peer into them and growling as they went.

All of them were looking for someone. Morgan was pretty sure she knew who.

This was familiar. She'd been here before. She slouched lower in her seat and tried not to breathe deeply.

"Morgan, act casual" whispered Sam softly.

"Yeah, I'll get right on that." she whispered back.

When transfixed by fear, the mind can do some funny things. As he sat there motionless, Sam noticed that not one of the "normal" people seemed to even notice any of the outrageous, terrifying things going on around them.

"Maybe that means that a swan knight really can pass unnoticed when he chooses to do so" he thought. "At some point, I'm going to owe Claud a big apology. That is, of course, assuming that he, I and Morgan make it out of here alive. Which is a pretty big assumption at this point."

Meanwhile, dramatic theme music started to play in Morgan's head. It was just her adrenalin cranking its way up to "Go – Baby – GO…" levels.

She saw a flash of color moving from the corner of her eye and had to keep a firm hold of her emotions to turn her head s–l–o–w–l–y, rather than whip it around to see what was happening. There was the disturbing sound of something enormous s–n–i–f–f–i–n–g at the car door that she was crouched down behind; and then a large body thumped up against the car door as something moved a little bit closer to them.

Morgan closed her eyes briefly and tried her best to use a mind frozen with fear to form some kind, any kind of a plan that meant survival for them all with at least half of their limbs intact. She was fond of her limbs, and her life as well, and she was sure that her passengers probably felt the same way about their own.

Then something happened that surprised her. Something she had not expected.

Claud softly and slowly leaned across from the passenger seat, gently grasping her arm and pulling her closer to him to whisper softly into her ear.

"Mein lady, to me you vill now please listen. Something mad, I am going to do. The villains' attention, I vill get, and vhen it I have, you both must run."

He smiled widely at her then, a bold but innocent smile far too full of confidence

"One boon to ask I have. If I cannot, I ask that to my people, my message you vill carry.

"Mein Unseelie enemies, those folk are," he said, pointing at the road ahead. "The ones who the princess took. The ones who my fellow svan knights slaughtered. The faces of these villains mark, that, in the future, to answer for these evil deeds, they may be called."

All this was said in only a few seconds.

"No! Stop! Stop him!" her mind screamed at her. "There are too many of them. A troop like this took his entire patrol down, and now he's going to take them all on alone, wounded as he is? This is madness!"

As if he could read her thoughts, Claud smiled again, sadly this time.

"Mein lady, I know that, vhile varriors you two are

not, full of courage your hearts are. I know that you do not vish to leave me alone to fight, but far bigger than the life of one single svan knight this is."

"My folk varriors born are. If they believe that de Mantelfiederfolk someone has wronged, on that people they vill var declare. I fear that someone my people are trying to deceive and against the wrong enemy them set."

"If I cannot, to them de truth you must tell. Brave in heart, you both are; brave in heart, but varriors not. Good sense it therefore is that to fight I must stay and, that with de truth for mein people, you must go."

"Mein sveet lady and you clever cat -zen, to run you must prepare." he said, and leaned away from her again.

She wanted to stop him. She desperately wanted to stop him; but she wasn't fast enough. Before she could do anything, Claud opened the car door.

Hard. Very, very hard; and something yelped and began to howl behind that door.

"Hal – lo!" shouted Claud, cheerfully and emerging quickly from the car. "Hal – lo!! I believe that some of you for me have been looking, yah?"

And the world all around them went dead silent for a minute.

Twenty- Eight
Swans Misled

When the princess' wedge had not returned from its' woodland ride at the expected hour, no one had thought anything of it at first. The swan princess was often impulsive and given to flights of fancy. It would not be the first time she was gone beyond the hour appointed. Her mother, leader and shaman of the flock, snorted, vexed as usual by her wayful and precocious eldest daughter.

As the sun rose and sank again across the vault of heaven and still there was no sign of her cygnet, the shaman queen grew first exasperated, and then gradually more alarmed. When twilight approached and there was still no sign of the missing swan folk, Hildreth withdrew to her tent and reached out to her spirits to locate her errant child.

The spirits returned, agitated. They had found no sign of her daughter, not in the spirit world nor on the physical planes.

Hildreth was even more alarmed now. Orders were given and warrior cobs leapt to horse to swiftly ride along paths that the princess habitually rode.

As they searched, at first there were no overt signs of trouble, only beautiful vistas and charming dells passing by as they rode. The riders galloped swiftly on, racing with the coming of darkness.

No signs of trouble. No signs of struggle. No signs of the princess.

It was deep into the shadows, deep into the heart of the woods, that they finally found signs of their people.

First, broken plants, and trampled earth. Footprints, many footprints. The signs of many men and horses locked in mortal conflict.

The riders slowed their progress then, watching

carefully for further indications of what had become of their people as well as any danger that might still be lurking. As they rode, they found more signs of conflict.

It was at a clearing at a crossroads deep in the woods that the attack had come; and the attack had been savage indeed. The clearing was trampled and was littered with the signs of conflict, and broken weapons, and a wounded horse, struggling desperately to stand on a leg that would no longer bear it.

And with the bodies of their missing fellow swan knights.

Now a swan is a dangerous creature. A swan is absolutely fearless in defense of its young and territory. A swan can even break a human being's arm with a single stroke of its' powerful wing.

And a warrior swan knight combines all of the fierceness of a normal swan with the wisdom, the strength and the cunning of a man – of a man trained from his birth to the perfection of the many skills of a warrior.

That being said, anything that could possibly lay waste to a squadron of swan warriors, even taken by surprise, must be something very dangerous indeed.

The leader of the swan wedge dismounted first, and cast about for clues. He gestured to his most skilled trackers to join him on the ground, to read the story that the battle signs had to tell.

One by one, they sought the faces of the dead. They listed them in their heads and in their hearts, mentally matching names of the dead with those who had ridden forth with the princess that morning. One by one, mentally naming each warrior lost to them.

All were gone – all but one warrior lost in death to them. He perhaps had crawled off into the brush to die or was even now dragging himself in the wake of his enemies.

Trying his best to follow them as any true swan warrior would.

For the swan princess was missing. Borne away into mystery. All they could do now was look for any signs that might lead them to her.

At their leader's command, the rest of the wedge dismounted. The groaning horse was examined and given its final peace. The bodies of their fellow swan knights were given due respect and gathered together in death as they had been in life. The warriors slowly fanned out and began to search intensely, looking for any possible indications that might lead them to their princess or the missing warrior.

As they moved further out of the clearing, they found tracks that led to frightened horses, ridden this morning by swan knights and now roaming free and frantic in the woods. The horses were glad to see a friendly face and came willingly into the keeping of the swans.

Back at the cross roads, the leader's brow furled in confusion. He had dead swan warriors. He had dead and missing horses. He had one warrior missing. He had one princess gone.

And he had not a sign of who or what had done it.

That was peculiar. The swan warriors were fierce warriors. Even if an enemy had taken them by surprise, there should be some sign of damage done by the swan knights to their foes.

Unless, of course, those enemies had taken care to clear such signs away with them. That was a curious thought indeed...

Just then, a cry went up from a warrior deep in the woods, and the leader lost track of the thought. Shaking his head, the leader moved swiftly join the warrior and see what he had found.

Behind a bush was a cloak of feathers. Crouching,

he carefully looked at it, seeking for anything it could tell him about what had gone before.

The cloak was caught there amongst the branches, loosely caught there as if it had fallen from a slowly moving horse. He gently disengaged it, carefully so he would not damage it or destroy any sign that it might have for him.

It was the princess' cloak; and it was clotted with blood.

This was bad. The princess was in the hands of her enemies and presumably helpless. Without her cloak, she was stripped of the powers she might otherwise use to break free.

And underneath the bush's lower branches, something lay on the ground glistened in the sun.

He bent down and looked under the bush. Half hidden by the leaves was a golden cloak pin. A brooch that bore the crest of the rulers of the high court of the Seelie sidhe.

The leader of the scouting party whistled under his breath. Well, this would certainly stir up trouble…

The high court of the sidhe had dominion over many of the enchanted folks – but the swan folk had always had their own culture and their own fiefdoms and had gone their own ways in the Lands that Lay Between. For the most part, the swan folk ignored the elven courts and the Sidhe high courts, whether Seelie or Unseelie, found the swan folk beneath their notice. They lived quite comfortably in mutual contempt of each other for much of the time, but a source of direct conflict such as this one could lead directly to a war.

This could be very bad indeed.

The leader of the scouting party shook his head and tucked the cloak of feathers and the brooch away in the leather bag that hung at his side. Important issues such as this should be brought to his leader as quickly as possible.

"Ho! Mount up!" he shouted to the swan knights, swinging back upon to his horse once more. Around him, the other swan warriors vaulted to their saddles, seizing the reins of the reclaimed horses loaded down with the bodies of their fallen fellow warriors. As one, they thundered out of the clearing, riding away from the cross roads, and back to the camp grounds of the swan folk.

Twenty-Nine
Sacrifice

The street was full- full of dark shadows and evil beasts and sinister figures; and Claud stood there in the midst of them like a single torch shining into darkness.

He reached down and detached something from his belt - a long rope with a metal dart attached to one end. He smiled and gestured with the dart at the ominous figures around him.

"All right! Vith me, who vants first to dance?"

There was a pause; and then all hell broke loose in the narrow streets. Dark hunds leaped, snarling and foaming, howling in their eagerness to get at him. Warriors drew eldritch weapons and circled around, looking for weakness. Lesser horrors skittered along the outskirts of the situation, looking for a handy opening- a tendon, an arm, an Achilles heel if possible.

Claud stood in the midst of them, smiling genially at them all.

With so much activity in the narrow street, it was only natural that some assailants would get in each other's' way. Hunds knocked heads together hard and fell back howling. Warriors fouled their fellows' weapons. There were so many enemies trying to reach Claud that they prevented each other from being efficient.

A more level playing field – and a more level playing field is better to play hard on.

Claud went to work. With a mighty shout, he began swing the rope in a semicircle, with the dart at the far end. The dart covered a growing arc, and where dart hit skin or hide, it drew blood.

Soon his opponents were not only withdrawing from each other but also from the cuts the dart inflicted on any being that dared to come close. As the arcs grew wider, the dart caused more damage until it traced a full circle, high and low, in a killing zone around the swan knight.

With the part of his mind not frozen with fear, Sam noted that, no matter how uncanny the adversaries of the blond Fiederfolk appeared, no matter how flamboyantly the swan knight moved, no matter how theatrical the combat became, the humans sitting in their cars took no notice.

"Drat! I **am** going to owe him an apology!" thought Sam. "How embarrassing! He really *does* have the ability to pass unseen."

Slouching down low in the shelter of her driver's seat, Morgan grabbed her purse and keys and eased the car door on her side open as quietly as she could. She slid out of the car with Sam following.

She might as well not have bothered being stealthy. All of the Unseelie attention was focused on the swan knight, who fought with a combination of confidence, competence and an excessively theatrical style seldom matched by any one person since the golden age of Hollywood. Morgan and Sam were able to easily slip away from the car and dash across the street into a sheltering alleyway without attracting unwelcome attention.

As space opened up, carved out by the hurtling dart, Claud began to change his tactics. Seizing the dart firmly in one hand, he cast it straight outwards towards his foes, still retaining his grasp on the rope's end. With every throw, the dart bit deep into Unseelie flesh, and, when he drew it back once more, it did even more damage.

Warriors were scrambling wildly for cover. Dark hunds were running here and there, howling hysterically. Claud was smiling broadly, doing what he'd been trained to do- create havoc amongst his foes and cause as much damage as he could.

Claud was doing well. Very well indeed.

Then, things changed.

A towering figure lunged into the open space before the swan knight, twisting to avoid the dart's point and reaching to grasp the rope behind it. With a powerful pull, the rope broke free of the swan knight's grasp, and dart and rope were lost to him.

Claud immediately unshipped paired hand axes from his belt; small but solid hatchet–like weapons with blades like stylized swans' wings. Holding the swan axes in a defensive position, Claud prepared himself to dance with his foes and make those facing him pay dearly for the pleasure of the process.

A thunderous voice rang out sharply.

"You idiots! You total idiots! Look at yourselves! You are doing all of his work for him! Your total lack of co-ordination and basic common sense are keeping you from doing him any harm and making it easy for him to cut you down like so many tassels of wheat! This is only one single wounded swan knight that you face, and he is making a total hash out of all of you!"

The dark and sinister heads of all of the various Unseelie snapped around, and they collectively looked abashed in the peculiar, uncanny way that only true Evil can. The dark hunds whined and slunk away to the edges of the melee, where they crouched somberly, snapping occasionally out of pique at a lesser tittering gremlin.

Claud took advantage of the Unseelie horde's momentary distraction to strike out with his hand axes at his nearest foes, always drawing blood. There was more than one yelp, groan or curse to be heard, and very soon, all of his enemies moved to a more respectful distance; but, even as they sidled away from the blond barbarian, their primary attention was still fixed firmly on the unseen thunderous voice.

"And now that I finally have all of your attention" the severe voice continued in a frustrated tone "let us just see, shall we, if we can actually act like something slightly like an evil menace for a moment or so, if that is not too much to ask of you all."

If there had ever been an evil way to shuffle one's feet, there would have been a whole lot of evil foot shuffling going on.

Claud tensed himself and prepared to charge his foes and sell his life for as high a price as he could manage, given the current rates of exchange. At the start of the fight, the opposition had been so disorganized that they'd gotten in their own way, but the mysterious voice was quickly taking that advantage away from him. Things would be getting more interesting soon.

Claud prepared to sell his life dearly, and Death itself began to circle round him, looking to buy what he had to sell.

From the shadowed alleyway, Morgan and Sam stopped for a moment and looked back at the battle. They had seen how, against all odds, Claud had been holding his own against his enemies and actually cutting into the ranks opposing him. For a few moments, they even had some hope that he might possibly come out of this combat alive.

But the Unseelie warriors took a breath, and began to co-ordinate their attacks, spurred on by the thunderous directions from the unseen voice. Dark hunds leaped in to harry the swan knight. Warriors staggered their efforts, leaving Claud always with one flank exposed and at risk as he turned to deal with the other side.

Claud fought more frantically than before. He was no longer smiling and began to lose ground before his enemies. Defending to one side of him, he took wounds from the other; and there was no safe wall he could reach to set his back against. Striking harder and faster, he began to sing loudly. Morgan had never heard such a song- a song so filled with power and strength and hope and despair.

And as Claud sang, he struck at his foes more and more fiercely, until they all fell back again for a moment,

But a moment,

Then, they all closed in again,

And the song ceased…

Thirty
Journeywork

From the moment that the tarot reader walked through the gates of the Seelie court, he knew there was something more than met the eye happening. Many of the members of the court were sick and more becoming so every minute, but there was more than simple illness at work here. People were dropping too quickly. The illness was spreading too rapidly, and it seemed to especially target people more critical to the defense of the court, such as the warriors and the leaders, as opposed to courtiers. The tarot reader could feel hostile magick at work here. As a shaman, he was trained to be aware of and deal with such things.

First things first- he and the palmist did triage, identifying those who were sickest, having beds moved to the great hall so it would be easier to observe and tend people and developed a working plan for anyone yet on their feet to help with taking care of the ill.

As soon as he could though, he whispered briefly in his partner's ear to tell her what he had observed and what he was doing. He then slipped away to a quiet side room where he could concentrate and see what he could do about the metaphysical aspects of the situation.

He settled himself comfortably, arms and legs uncrossed. (Going out of body and coming back to find your limbs asleep was not something you would do more than once.) He closed his eyes and took a breath, and then another and then a third. He could feel his body relaxing as it had been taught, preparing for journey work.

He launched himself into the world of spirit.

There was a rush of color, and, as things settled, he found himself in the middle world. On this journey, it looked like a forest and he was facing an immense oak tree.

"The lower world is the place to look for diseases and also a great place to meet with my spirit guides, so down we go." he thought.

With that, he saw an opening in the tree trunk. Looking in, he found a staircase spiraling downwards. "Convenient" he thought and began to descend the stairs.

In time, he came to the bottom of the stairs and an opening into a different forest. He stepped out of the tree and walked forwards, looking around for the next step of his journey. It was therefore no surprise when a few minutes later, he heard someone quietly hissing at him from the bushes.

"psst. psst, Hey you!..."

The tarot reader peered through the shrubs and found himself looking directly into the eyes (one blue, one green) of Coyote, his guide. The tarot reader stifled his initial startle and stepped through the branches to meet with him.

Coyote sat back on his haunches and grinned at him in a friendly fashion. He tipped his head to the side and let his tongue loll out slightly, looking far more foolish than he actually was.

The tarot reader braced himself internally. Coyote was a wise and helpful guide, but he was also a trickster. Sometimes he liked to make people work for their knowledge. If he was acting playful, this might be one of those times.

"So, you've come to see your old friend, eh?" said Coyote. "Are you here for knowledge or just for fun?"

"Much as I'd love to spend the day with you, I'm here on an urgent mission in regards to a question beyond my skill." said the tarot reader. "We have a sudden bout of illness in the Seelie court and it stinks to the heavens of maleficent magick. Unfortunately, I can't nail down the nature or the source of the pestilence. I was hoping that you might be willing to turn your attention to the situation and give me some input on what and who is causing it, and what I can do about it."

"Flattery will get you everywhere" grinned Coyote "especially when it's a situation that affects the balance of power in the lands that lie beyond. Just a minute please…"

Coyote closed his eyes and concentrated. The tarot reader could feel the wave of power rising as his guide reached out for the knowledge he'd been asked for. There was a moment of silence and then Coyote opened his eyes

"Well that's curious" said Coyote, a puzzled look on his face. "I can tell that you are right- your pestilence has a magickal source and cannot by healed by physical means alone- but I cannot see who is spreading this illness or why."

Coyote scratched his ear in puzzlement, confronted by a problem he could not instantly solve. "I will keep looking for answers" he said "but you will need to act quickly if you are to save those in your care, and you will need an approach that includes both body and spirit. Once I have more information, I will contact you, but do not wait on me because the answers may come too late for some."

"Just keep in mind" he added "that whoever is doing this is most powerful if he can hide himself from my sight, and that he evidently holds an immense grudge against the Seelie court. Take care that you do not place yourself in his path. I should miss our visits."

"I would miss them too" said the tarot reader rising to his feet "and I thank you, as always, for your counsel. I had best head back then. I have left my wife tending the sick alone."

Coyote chuckled. "By all means then, go" he said "she is a good woman, but if you leave her doing all the work too long, you will surely hear about it afterwards. Go. Go."

The tarot reader turned and walked briskly back to

the door way in the tree and climbed the steps to the middle world. He then took the three deep breaths, set the intention to return to where he had started and felt himself falling back into his body.

Once he had grounded himself, he stood and returned to the main hall, where beds were still being set up and filled. He passed behind the palmist and bent to whisper in her ear about what he had learned (and what he had not) from his guide.

She shook her head and continued to set up the sick beds.

Thirty-One
Sam and Morgan Flee

Tears ran down her face as Morgan ran down the street, Sam at her heels. The sounds of battle slowly faded behind her as the sound of her breathing increased.

Claud…

He had sacrificed himself for a principle – that truth was bigger than one man's life. He had sacrificed himself for his people – to see that they would get the information they needed to survive and possibly save their princess in the process. He had sacrificed himself for Sam and Morgan, to see them safely away.

She'd never seen anything like that before.

Now, his mission was their mission, because he'd sacrificed himself in order for them to escape from the Unseelie and could therefore no longer fulfill it.

Morgan ran on, weeping.

Footsteps pattering, leaping behind them, but not far enough behind. Heavy panting echoing off of buildings. Elusive shadows reflecting off lights in their wake.

Claud had sacrificed himself for them, but it might not have been enough.

Something was following them- or somethings. From the sound of it, it seemed to be more than one.

This was worrisome. They'd do their best in a scrimmage, but, as Claud had said, they weren't really fighters. They'd left their only martial protection behind them while they did their best to escape with the information he'd charged them to bring to his people. He'd thought that the Unseelie would all focus on him and disregard the two of them as being of no importance.

Evidently, this was not the case. They were still

121

pursued, although, from the sound of it, only by a small group of their enemies; and the only weapons they had between them were Morgan's oversized bag, and Sam's teeth, claws and sardonic wit.

Not a good thing by any definition of good. Worse yet, no signs of sanctuary in the offing.

Morgan had been working out and was in better shape than she'd been on their previous adventure, but she was still beginning to run out of steam. Her breath hissed audibly between her teeth, her muscles began to burn, and she began to fall behind the running golden cat.

Sam looked back and saw her lagging further and further behind him. He instantly reversed himself and dashed quickly back to her, turning and pacing her steps as she ran and wheezed and ran again. The footsteps of their–unseen pursuers echoed behind them in the inky darkness, coming closer and closer all of the time.

"No way this will work" said Sam, suddenly. "Stop and drop your purse! Now!"

Bewildered, Morgan skidded to a stop and dropped her purse. Sam leapt upon it like a cheetah on a gazelle and quickly pawed the top open. Reaching in, he pulled out the napkin that he'd placed in the purse earlier and deposited it carefully on the ground.

Meanwhile, the sounds of pursuit came closer and closer.

Sam carefully nosed the napkin open, revealing four little crystals. One by one, he took a crystal in his mouth and dashed to each of the cardinal points of the compass- first east, then south, then west, and finally north.

Morgan watched the golden cat nervously. She could hear that something was almost on them, and whatever it was wasn't good.

Sam moved quickly back to the first crystal, the one

in the east. Reaching it, he sat by it in a stylized cat position, paws together, back straight, head alert and ears listening, tail wrapped carefully and formally around his paws. Ideal position attained, he spoke.

"Guardians of the watch towers of the east, I bid you welcome to our circle and I ask for your protection now from all things of evil and of darkness."

Though sorely distracted at the moment, Morgan thought she saw a brief flicker in the air around them.

Sam arose fluidly then and trotted swiftly clockwise to the next crystal, the one in the south. Again, he assumed a posture of formal cat respect.

"Guardians of the watch towers of the south, I bid you welcome to our circle and I ask for your protection now from all things of evil and of darkness."

The flicker caught Morgan's eye again, stronger this time than before. The sounds were almost upon them

Once more rising and moving, Sam continued clockwise to the crystal in the west. Once more he sat respectfully and spoke.

Morgan closed her regular eye so she could watch her furry companion with her seeing eye. A stream of light followed behind Sam as he moved to the western crystal.

"Guardians of the watch towers of the west, I bid you welcome to our circle and I ask for your protection now from all things of evil and of darkness."

There was a scrabbling at the far end of the alley and Morgan looked up, only to see three dark hunds rapidly barreling down the confined space at them, followed by several lesser goblins. Her mind froze with terror.

Sam's head snapped up, taking note of the incoming adversaries. He dashed madly towards the final crystal, the one in the north, as death hurtled down on them. Reaching it, he sat and took his position as carefully as if he had all the time in the world.

"Guardians of the watch towers of the north," said the golden cat "I bid you welcome to our circle and I ask for your protection now from all things of evil and of darkness."

The massive dogs were almost upon them now, huge and hungry and fierce beyond comprehension. Morgan's mind was still frozen. She picked up her heavy purse in desperation, preparing to swing it in their defense.

Sam made a final clockwise dash, ending at the eastern crystal where he had first begun his circle. He seated himself carefully one final time.

"The circle is closed. So mote it be!" he shouted. His voice boomed and echoed, impossibly bigger than his normal speaking voice.

The sound filled the alley way.

And a circle of Light sprang up. Light passing from crystal to crystal. Light connecting in a circle of Light. Light forming a dome around and over them. Light flooding the world around them

The dark hunds arrived just as the dome of Light rose.

Howling, snarling, slathering, the dark hunds charged them, howling wildly as they threw themselves upon the woman and the cat.

And were driven back by the Light.

As the dark hunds hit the dome, sparks flew and the Light surged brighter. Morgan almost had to squeeze her seeing eye shut because the increasing Light was so overwhelming and painful. The hunds were thrown backwards by the impact with the dome of Light, crying out and howling with pain. Smoke arose from burning places on their hides. They tumbled backwards, curling into tight little knots of misery.

And lesser horrors gathered around them, chittering

anxiously or cackling with glee at the misfortune of their fellows.

Braced for the impact of the massive canine bodies, Morgan straightened up. The Light shone around her, shone around them both, creating a safe ground, free from evil influences and energy.

They were safe. At least for the moment, they were safe. It was a long moment, which was also a good thing.

"Remember when I said that we should send a fruit basket to the guy that created those wards?" said Sam. "Well, I'm upping that order to flowers, at the very least."

Morgan smiled weakly at him.

The dark hunds had recovered their composure in only a few short minutes and began prowling around the outside of the dome of Light, growling fiercely and ferociously at them. They started to test the dome, poking at it with their noses, and yelping as the Light burned them once more.

"I hope those wards hold." said Sam nervously.

The dark hunds were gradually working themselves up into a frenzy, snarling and circling and lunging harder and harder at the edges of the circle. Every time one lunged at the circle, sparks flew up, and the hound yelped and quickly withdrew; but every time, the Light dimmed slightly and every time, the beasts drew closer and closer to breaking through the barrier that was blocking them from their prey.

Morgan and Sam huddled closer and closer together in the very center of the circle, waiting to see if their defenses would hold.

The dark hunds continued to circle, testing the wards again and again with more force each time. At last, one of them pressed just hard enough that one paw briefly crossed the barrier, before pain and burning made him withdraw it.

The beasts howled together in triumph, as Morgan

and Sam braced themselves and braced themselves for the moment when the wards would fail.

And then a figure came around the corner, into the Light reflected from the wards.

He was small but solid, barely larger than a human child, but by the points of his ears and the set of his features, clearly one of the fae. He walked briskly but confidently, like someone out about his daily routine. He was a hob, and he was smiling.

Morgan recognized him. On her last trip through the lands of the sidhe, she was separated from Sam for part of her journey. While on her own, she had run across him being attacked by a pack of small and malicious Unseelie sidhe. She'd never liked bullies and seeing this made her angry which overcame her fear. She'd rushed at his tormentors, striking out with feet and fists, and the fierceness of her amateur attack had been enough to put his opponents to flight and to save his life.

This situation was different. She wasn't strong enough to vanquish the dark hunds on her own, and he was smaller and less powerful than she was. He would surely die if he stayed

"RUN!" she shouted frantically. "Run! Get away while you can."

The small sidhe continued to advance and to smile.

The dark hunds turned to face him. Their ears perked up and their tails wagged for just a moment. Here was fresh and easy meat – unprotected and far too small to fight them. They started to slink slowly towards him, enjoying the hunt and waiting for him to cry out, to show fear or to flee, which would only add to the fun.

The small sidhe reached deep into his satchel. He pulled out a horn-beautiful and intricate, covered with complicated designs of leafy vines intertwined with Celtic knotwork. He smiled once more as savage hounds stalked towards him, stiff legged and growling fiercely, and then he brought the horn to his lips.

He blew the horn. Once. Just once.

But the sound of one blast of the horn echoed around them, swelling and growing larger with every moment. Sound, bouncing off buildings and cars and returning, stronger and stronger and stronger. Sound, sweet but swelling, swelling in sound and volume and power until Morgan cried out in pain and fear and awe, crouching down and clapping her hands over her ears to deaden the noise.

The dark hunds recoiled, cringing and crying out in pain as the sound hit them forcibly again and again. They fell to the ground, writhing and rolling about in their torment. They howled and they screeched and pawed at their ears in their distress, clawing at them until the skin was broken and the blood flowed down.

The lesser horrors fled, holding their hands to their ears and crying out their distress aloud.

And still the sound persisted, growing and swelling and rebounding once more.

With her fingers now seated firmly in her ears, Morgan found herself uncomfortable, but no longer in pain. Looking at Sam, she found him crouched on the ground at her feet, head flat on the pavement and paws clapped firmly over his own ears, but also not showing signs of pain.

Turning her attention to the dark hunds, she saw that, while she and Sam were uncomfortable, the pain the dogs were feeling seemed to continue to grow and increase without ceasing. She almost felt sorry for the gaunt and fearsome ravagers. Almost, but not quite. After all, they had been ready to rip herself and her furry companion to shreds

Looking back at the hob who was now standing just outside of their circle, she was surprised to find him still

127

smiling, horn at lips, and showing no signs of discomfort whatsoever.

He inhaled deeply.

He pursed his lips.

And he screwed up his face and put his all into one more blast. A blast that shook the buildings around them. A blast that struck through right to the core of Morgan's very being. A blast that sent the dark hunds, screaming and crying and howling, fleeing headlong from the alley with ears down flat and tails tucked tightly between their legs.

He removed the horn from smiling lips and said something.

"What?" screamed Morgan, and then she remembered and removed her fingers from her ears.

"What?" she shouted again and startled herself. Despite the blast of sound she'd just experienced, she evidently hadn't been deafened permanently.

"What?" she said a third time at normal volume.

"I said…" said the hob "…hello. How nice to see you again, although not under these circumstances, of course…"

Morgan paused and then took a deep breath.

"How nice to see you as well" she said, feeling a bit off center. "And thank you for the rescue. We were getting a little worried there."

"Oh, no worries, no worries, my dear" said the hob.

"I could see that you two were doing splendidly just as you were. I just thought that I might like to lend a hand, owing you as much as I do."

Sam had removed his paws from his ears and was grooming himself and eyeing the hob curiously.

"I think we met briefly at the coronation of the new king. Nice to see you again." he said. "So, what's with the horn? Are you specializing in pest removal now?"

The hob smiled shyly at the cat and then turned back

to Morgan again.

"After you saved my life last year" he said earnestly. "I decided that I needed to find some way of defending myself from such unpleasant situations. I applied myself more seriously to my research, and, with time, have created this lovely horn, which is very helpful on occasions such as this. An effective deterrent but also non-lethal."

He smiled brightly, having in his mind explained everything very clearly.

At this point, Morgan had about a thousand questions at the least, but Sam intervened.

"I think I've heard about horns like these. Am I correct in thinking" asked the golden cat carefully "that the horn is a temporary solution, then?"

The hob smiled brightly. "Why yes!" he said, pleased that the cat seemed to understand his work

He thought and his face grew more serious "…which means that soon they will all be back. This horn will not blow another such blast soon, which means that you should be on your way quickly, and I should be on my own way as well."

He smiled again. "We really must get together some time in the future when we have more time to talk." he said.

"It's a date" said Morgan, still feeling somewhat dazed.

"Sure thing, but for now, let's beat feet" added Sam.

"Then fare you well, and I hope to see you again in the future in more pleasant circumstances" said the hob, bowing slightly. He tucked his horn back into his sack and was quickly away again, leaving Sam and Morgan in the alley, looking at each other.

"We need someplace safe to hole up and figure out what's our next step." Morgan said.

"Agreed" said Sam "and more than that, we need to be away from here when those bozos come back. Let me take down the wards and then let's go."

He dashed to the northern ward and positioned himself quickly but meticulously. "Guardians of the watch towers of the north" he said "we thank you for your protection from all things of evil and of darkness. Go if you must, stay if you will." Moving briskly counterclockwise, he thanked the guardians of the west, the south and the east, and then ended with "the circle is open."

And with that, they gathered up the wards and went.

Thirty- Two
Bad News

Hildreth, the swan shaman, was waiting when the warrior band returned. Dismounting, the leader of the wedge strode up to her, reaching into his leather bag.

"Mein shaman queen! Something terrible, it has happened. Our people, ve have found, but, one knight and your daughter missing are, and the rest have all been killed."

The swan shaman roared with rage.

"Who has this done?" she demanded.

"Your daughter's feather cloak ve found" said the soldier, holding up the blood-stained mantle "and beneath it this brooch was. Seelie symbols it bears.

The shaman seized the bloody bundle of feathers from him, and stared at it for a moment, her face unreadable.

"But, something strange there was …" he added, still holding out the golden cloak clasp.

She froze him in mid-sentence with a look.

"To ride, yourselves hold ready..." she said finally, still staring at the cloak. "Vith the spirits, I must now consult."

Turning on her heel, she strode into the vision lodge, leaving her warriors troubled and confused.

Thirty- Three
Dowsing for Swan Folks

They had hopped a bus, jumped floors using elevators in several tall buildings and walked through the perfume counters at a certain department store in an attempt to throw any hunters off their trail, and were now hiding in plain sight in a very public food court at a local mini mall downtown.

"So how do we find the swan folk anyway?" said Morgan. "You got any ideas?

"Not a one" said Sam from his place in her oversized purse. "The plan was the swan knight was gonna give us directions, but that's kinda fallen apart. Got anything to eat out there?"

Morgan slipped a quarter of her tuna sandwich to him, while she thought a moment. "I wonder... I wonder if I could possibly find them by dowsing with my pendulum." she asked, hesitantly.

"Well, they're not a set of car keys" said Sam, "but, what the heck – give it a try."

There was a tourist map of the city lying on the empty table next to her. She reached over and took it and pulled her moss agate pendulum out of the side pocket of her purse. Opening the map, she dangled the pendulum carefully above it.

It began to quiver with eagerness.

Morgan smiled at it. She remembered how well it had worked in finding those car keys and playing hot and cold with objects that Sam had hidden for her. She felt sure that they were on the right track to finding the swan folk.

She started with three classic questions she'd been taught were often used by dowsers.

"Can I dowse for the location of the swan folk" she

asked first, asking whether conditions were appropriate for such work. Then "Should I dowse for the swan folk?", inquiring whether it was a good idea to be doing this. And finally, "May I dowse for the swan folk?", asking whether those energies and spirits that do such work were willing to work with her now.

"Yes!" swayed the pendulum, and "yes!" and "yes!" again.

Having received clearance, Morgan asked the next question. "Where can I find the swan folk?"

And the pendulum was immediately pulled to a specific place on the map.

Thirty- Four
Hidden in Both Worlds

The swan shaman sat alone in the stillness of the vision lodge, looking intently at her daughter's bloody swan cloak. She had already tried twice to link with her daughter, using the cloak as a connection to her child, but had had no success.

But, when at first you don't succeed, try, try again- and three was a magick number...

She focused her attention on the cloak, and set an intention to find her child, living or dead. She closed her eyes, took a deep breath and then another, and dropped into shamanic journey. She felt her body relax in preparation for traveling into the world of spirit. She focused her energy and separated spirit from body, to travel to the middle world and meet with her spirit guide.

The physical world fell away and her spirit soured into the aether.

She found herself in the middle world, sitting beside a blue and tranquil pool. Looking up, she could see an immense swan flying slowly downwards towards her- the Swan of swans, her totemic guide.

The swan landed in the pool and glided towards her. Hildreth stood and waded into the pond to meet her, facing her guide and looking deeply into its eyes. "My daughter Ariella missing is. Her I cannot find." she said. "To you I come for help to ask."

The swan was still for a minute, and then reared up, flapping it's wings fiercely. "I cannot see her!..." a voice came in her head "She has been ringed round with many cunning magicks to hide her along the spirit ways. "

"This much I can tell you though" the swan's voice continued "she is as yet alive and, with sufficient time, we

135

might be able to find a way to untangle the spells that conceal her. I fear though that we do not have that time to spare. If you do not find her soon, I cannot guarantee that she will survive."

"I regret that I have not been able to help you more at this time. I will continue to try to see past the walls that conceal her. And you, you must go now to try to find her in different ways…"

The swan lunged at Hildreth, pushing her fiercely. The swan shaman felt her spirit falling backwards and plunging down, down, down…

Until she fell into her body once more

She took a deep breath, and another.

Her daughter was alive. Ariella was alive.

But she had no way to find her.

Her fear for her daughter turned to rage- rage that someone dared to take her child from her like this. The rage grew within her and she roared with anger

She could not find her daughter. Her spirit guides could not find her daughter.

But still she had one clue- the Seelie brooch that had been found with her daughter's feather cloak.

She surged to her feet and strode out of the vision lodge as quickly as she had entered it. Her tribe was gathered outside of the lodge with worried faces, apprehensive about what her screams might mean.

Her lead scout approached her, still offering the Seelie broach. "About this, something strange there was." he began…

"To strangeness, no heed we shall pay" snarled his ruler. "If the stinking Shee think my daughter they can steal and our varriors slay, they should differently learn. Them ve shall go and teach!'"

The scout startled and swallowed what he had been

about to say. Her other followers shouted and raised their blades. They were going to harrow the Seelie Court, reclaim their princess and regain their honor.

There was a sound of preparations to ride.

Thirty-Five
Communication Block

They had been following the guidance of the pendulum when they first encountered the swan patrols, watching for strangers in the surrounding hills. They were brought under heavy guard into the encampment of the Mantelfiederfolk, up to the biggest in the circle of nomads' tents. Morgan noticed the camp was busy with warriors moving quickly to and fro, gathering weapons, taking down tents and saddling horses.

The guards threw back the flap of the tent and gestured roughly for them to step through into the dimness beyond. Bowing her head lower to enter, Morgan stepped in with Sam close at her heels.

It was dim and warm within the massive tent, and Morgan blinked to better focus. Looking around, she found herself in a scene of barbaric splendor, with wild looking blond warriors gathered around a central fire.

An impressive looking woman stood directly opposite her. She was strong and muscular with a presence that dominated the room and the people around her. She was dressed in soft white buckskins, trimmed with dangling thongs with bits of stone and bone and fur. She had a wealth of necklaces clasped about her neck, necklaces of amber, crystals and amulets varied and mysterious. She was mantled in a massive feather cloak with an intricate heavy iron clasp.

Morgan closed her regular eye and looked around her, using the eye of seeing alone. There was magick everywhere here! Magick in the cloaks of feathers. A faint glimmer of magick in each of the people seated within the tent. Most of all, magick shone from the powerful woman standing before Morgan. Magick twinkled from every little token or amulet tied to her garment. Magick shone from each and every necklace that she wore. Magick burst from her person itself, and she shone a hundredfold more brightly than any one of her followers.

As she looked, Morgan could also see faint, wispy, transparent figures around her. Figures of people and of animals. They ran to and fro around her. They reached for her with hand or paw. They stood beside her and tried to whisper in her ear.

And they seemed agitated.

Morgan opened her regular eye, so that she was seeing in the physical world once more. All of the brightness, all of the spirits vanished from her sight.

All of those present turned to look at Morgan, and she suddenly felt very small and self-conscious.

"Hail, Hildreth!" cried the leader of their escort. "Approaching our camp, this woman and cat vere found. For your attention and judgement, they are therefore before you brought. The woman claims that a message for you from one of our people she bears. No proof she has that this story is to be believed."

"I…" Morgan started.

"Alt!" shouted the leader of the escort. "unless our leader permits, you shall not speak."

Morgan bit her tongue.

Hildreth looked at her suspiciously.

"One of us, you are not." she said "vith the Fiederfolk, nothing to do you have. Yet to us you come, vith a story to tell. To someone like you, vhy should ve even listen?"

Morgan paused and looked at the leader of the swan people. Was this her time to speak? She decided she needed to take the opening, lest Claud's truth never got told at all.

"Because I'm here to speak for one of you" she said emphatically. "One who cannot speak for himself. I speak for Claud of the Mantelfiederfolk. He charged us to come to find you and bring you the truth about the attack on your warriors and the kidnapping of the swan princess. He sent me to tell you that the people who attacked them, who killed his fellows and took the princess, were a group of Unseelie sidhe. He was sorely wounded during the attack but escaped from them; and they pursued him because he was the only living witness to who really did this."

"As he fled, he came to my house. I gave him sanctuary, and, because he was badly wounded, came with him when he tried to return to you. As we traveled, we were set upon by the same Unseelie warriors. He told me that they had attacked his party and charged me to remember their faces. I became a witness for the Fiederfolk - witness to who killed your people and took your maiden."

"I fear he has given his life in our defense. He told us to flee while he held the enemy back, and he charged me to find his people and to bear his truth to you if he was unable to do so himself."

"so, here I am…" concluded Morgan.

One of the counselors looked thoughtful. "You know" he said "that is the kind of heroic foolishness that of Claud I vould expect…"

They all thought about that for a moment. Some of them even nodded their heads, and Morgan began to feel hopeful.

A minute later, her hopes were dashed.

Hildreth exploded, shamanic amulets rattling as she surged to her feet.

"Nonsense this is! Lying you are!" she shouted. "The truth this is not! No evidence to support your story you have! There is not a vay on the earth that a Fiederfolk warrior would from someone like you need help. You here come and expect that any silly tale you can tell and that ve vill as truth it accept."

"Ve know for a fact that our varriors vere all slain, and that none of them escaped, and that mein daughter the princess vas taken. Ve know that this evil thing by members of the Seelie court vas done! Yah! _Proof_ absolute ve have!"

The head of her warriors gestured wildly.

"Mein lady, Hildreth" he said urgently. "A point! The body of Claud ve did not find ven the rest of our varriors ve found…"

"ACH!" she shouted, cutting him off. "No proof she has that true her tale is. Towards the Seelie court the evidence points as those who have us wronged."

"Since the mark of the Seelie court clearly upon her is, ve can only think that she has been sent to us to distract and mislead. Vell, the Mantelfiederfolk are not fools to so easily be misled." Hildreth raged. "Stupid ve are not, and vith our enemies, ve know how to deal."

"For all of the evil done to us, a blood price in full ve vill have. Vith our Seelie enemies, to var ve vill go. If ve have to, the very gates of the Seelie court down ve vill break, that the vergild that ve are owed ve vill take."

"And to keep our enemies close vell ve know. So, you ve shall secure and, once the courts of Seelie ve have taken, then vith you as vell ve shall deal."

"Take them away!" she ordered, gesturing at them, and turned her back, indicating that she was finished with them. Some of her counselors looked troubled, but no one raised a word in opposition.

And then the guards closed in on them both.

Thirty- Six
A Question of Blood

Ariella found herself lying on the stone floor of a deep and cavernous room. The walls were roughhewn and the ceiling soared out of sight in the shadows. Along the walls were shelves and cabinets, piled high with books and tools and many curious things. She lay within a massive circle scribed into the floor, circled round with many esoteric and occult symbols.

She could feel someone approaching her from behind. Could feel someone standing over her body and looking closely at her as she lay on the floor, helpless.

The sorcerer moved into her visual field. He was tall and lean to the point of gauntness, yet muscular. His eyes were touched with more than a hint of madness. He bent down and caught hold of her chin, lifting her head so she had no choice but to look into those eyes.

"Interesting." he said.

He let her head drop. Turning away, he began to clear the surface of a large marble table.

"I suppose you're wondering what is about to happen to you…" he said off-handedly as he worked.

Bound and gagged, Ariella could only nod.

"It is only fair to let you know, I suppose." he said, taking a large pile of books to the bookcase. "Our local Unseelie lord has had you taken captive, purely to stir your people up and turn them as a weapon against the oh-so–innocent Seelie court. The ensuing battle will weaken both sides, leaving them vulnerable to Unseelie attack."

"He has had you delivered to me, to keep you hidden from any who might rescue you and unmask the deception he is practicing upon your people. And for you, dear princess, I have plans of my own," he added, turning to face her "many plans indeed."

"I have heard the stories of your people." he said, moving slowly towards her. "I have heard what happened after the brothers were saved, and how they missed their lives as swans. I have heard how they sought to regain the power to transform themselves into the great white birds. "

"And I have heard how they succeeded."

"Because your ancestors had been cursed into the bodies of swans, the memory of the swan lingered on in them, long after the curse was lifted. The "shape of the swan" was in their blood, and that "shape of the swan" was what allowed them to regain the ability to transform at will."

"That ability has been passed down from the six brothers unto their blood descendants even to this very day, allowing their descendants to also become swans."

He brought his face down closer to hers. "The "shape of the swan" is in your blood, little princess. And soon, when I drain that precious blood from your body and take it into mine, the "shape of the swan" shall be in my blood, too." he whispered.

Ariella stared at him horrified.

"It shall be in my blood as well" he said, his voice gradually rising with excitement "and I too shall fly! I too shall be able to take the form of a swan, and the powers that go with such a form! And why stop there? If I could change into a swan, then why not into other birds and beasts? Why not be able to be whatever I wish to be?"

He began to laugh. Euphorically. Hysterically.

Ariella lay there looking at him, her mind racing.

"He does not know that, to the process, mein feather cloak essential is. Very disappointed, he is going to be vhen mein blood he drinks, and it does not for him vork." she thought abstractedly.

Her mind focused, and she mentally slapped herself.

Hard.

"Ariella, you little fool" she thought "of vat are you thinking? Vat do you care if happy this accursed evil sorcerer is?"

"He vants your people to harm!"

"He vants your blood to drink!"

"He vants your powers to take and them for EVIL use!!!"

"And as a varrior princess of a proud people, your job is everything you can do his evil plans to block."

"…and if, from like a tankard of mead drinking you, you can him keep, a good thing that also is." she mentally added.

The sorcerer turned away again as he continued to clear his work space.

"If you will just wait there for a moment, my gentle princess" said the sorcerer "I will prepare a more fitting and comfortable space for you."

"My gentle princess? Oh my," she thought "myself or my people, most certainly he does not know."

She began once again to subtly stretch and worry at her bonds, straining against the ropes and testing them from every angle possible. Her muscles cramped, her skin was abraded, her circulation decreased and she developed pins and needles in various parts of her body, but she continued to work at the restraints.

And the ropes began to stretch ever so slightly.

Spirits renewed, she stretched harder in the direction that the ropes were giving way...

Thirty- Seven
An Unexpected Ally

Sam and Morgan lay uncomfortably piled in a corner of a tent. Her hands and feet were bound, and he was captive in a tightly woven net made of cords with iron interwoven into them. (Evidently the Fiederfolk had dealt with small but clever beasts often enough that they had developed a specific remedy.)

"Sam, do I really truly have the mark of the Seelie court clearly on me?" asked Morgan plaintively.

"Well, duh! Of course you do." said Sam. "Do you remember that ceremony when the royals embraced you and kissed you on the forehead? Well…"

"Was that it?" asked Morgan. "because I thought that was purely ceremonial."

"Nope. Not so." said Sam cheerfully. "Leaves a mystic mark on your forehead for those that can see it to indicate you are under the protection of the Seelie court."

"O. k. Seems like it's working more like the Black Spot than any real protection though." said Morgan. "I can see that I'm going to have to use my eye of seeing from now on when I'm washing my face."

"Jumping subjects here, can you get loose?" Sam whispered.

"Let's see, shall we?" replied Morgan. She strained against her bonds but to no avail-the more she fought, the tighter they became.

"Evidently not. I knew I should have ordered that program on escape acts while I still had the chance." said Morgan, deciding to stop before she pulled a muscle. "How about you, Sam?"

Sam tensed his muscles and tried to stretch himself out to gain play in the net. Unfortunately, the net had been wrapped so tightly around him that he couldn't get any leeway. He changed his tactics and tried to gnaw on the strands of the net in front of him. The net proved too tough, leaving him panting and a bit tooth sore. The swan who had tied them up had certainly known his business.

"No joy here either." said Sam. "You know that heap of trouble I said we were in before? Well, double it!"

They heard quiet footsteps approaching the door to the tent.

"And what dazzling new bit of excitement have the fates now laid on for our entertainment?" asked Sam rhetorically.

A young girl with a very long sharp knife held tightly in both tiny hands stepped carefully through the tent flap.

"O.k. Sorry I asked." thought the cat.

The girl was slender and delicate, with milk pale skin, light blue eyes and long hair so blond as to be almost white. She was barely out of childhood with a look upon her face too solemn for her apparent years. The knife was very large, so large it almost seemed beyond her strength to carry it at all, let alone use it.

Sam and Morgan held their breaths and held very still in the corner. There was no way of telling what business this girl was on, and no good purpose in drawing attention to themselves as they lay there, bound and helpless before her.

The girl turned towards them, pale eyes curious and inquisitive but unreadable. Evidently, she was not here for anything else. Strong emotions played across her face.

She came towards them slowly but steadily. She squatted down on a pile of multi-colored bundles beside them and looked at them for a long moment. The knife quavered gently in her hands, as she toyed with it.

Morgan and Sam tried very hard to not think about what she might have brought the knife for.

There was a $v - e - r - y$ $l - o - n - g$ moment of silence, as the young girl eyed them both thoughtfully.

"Vat I thought you vould be, not at all you are." the girl remarked.

They stopped and thought about that for a moment.

"No?" asked Morgan finally, in a cautiously neutral tone. "Well, what were you expecting, then?"

"Not exactly sure, I am" said the young girl emphatically, gesturing with her knife. "Maybe someone a bit taller or more heroic looking?"

"After all of this time, I should really better know." she continued, amused with herself. "Of your coming, I saw. I know that, like the fairy tales, this is not."

Surprised, both Morgan and Sam nodded their heads as best they could.

"Anyway, I am here to say that vat you said, I believe, even if mein flock does not." said the girl. "To the spirits, I have spoken. They tell me that true your vords are, and on a righteous undertaking you go."

"And, hoo boy, for a big misunderstanding, mein flock heading is. Mein name is Estelle, and on your quest I am here to help."

"You are?" asked Sam inquisitively. "then what's with the cutlass there?"

"Vell, you don't think vith mein fingers alone that I can get you loose, do you?" asked the pale swan girl in an exasperated tone. "Very big ropes those are and little tiny fingers these are, mein fuzzy little friend. So, let us see vhat it is for you that ve can do."

She bent down first over the cat and brought the knife slowly down at him. Sam did his best not to flinch as the massive blade passed behind his back, and Estelle began sawing at the net.

"But aren't there lots of guards outside of the tent

149

flap there?" asked Morgan, straining against her own ropes and wincing at the increasing constriction that she was creating. "Won't they miss us? Won't they notice that you're cutting us loose?"

"Oh nein, nein, nein." said Estelle calmly, continuing to cut. "To var vith your friends at the Seelie court, they are all of them preparing to go. They think that the court has our varriors slain and Ariella, mein sister the svan princess, captive taken. Ven mein folk to var go, about anything else they do not much thinking do."

"Actually, come of it to think, that is one of the vays in vich from the rest of mein flock I different am." she said, thoughtfully stopping cutting for a moment to examine this concept more closely.

Sam waited for a long moment or two. "I'm glad to hear it" the golden cat finally said. "Could you keep on cutting though? They're wearing nets tighter this year than I'm really comfortable with."

Estelle looked startled and started sawing away at his bonds again.

"Oh, yah" she said. "you and your lady friend out of here ve must get. Places to go you have got, and people to see, and not any time for getting behind, nein?"

The tough strands of the net parted at this point, and, with just a little wriggling, Sam was able to free himself. Estelle then turned to Morgan, carefully cutting at the tightened ropes.

"You know," said Estelle excessively casually "they say that everything in life a price has, nein?"

Sam looked at Morgan, still bound. Morgan looked at Sam. They both looked at Estelle.

"Here it comes" said Sam. "The hook."

Estelle blushed a bit but kept cutting.

"Nein" she said "no hook there is. A request only.

150

The spirits tell me that in the vorld right now there is an evil force at vork; and between mein people and yours that it is trying trouble up to stir. Of this, my people I have tried my best to tell, but vith anger at evil already done, they are filled. vith rage, their ears are blocked, and me they cannot hear."

"The truth you are telling, they vill not hear. Our varrior you vere trying to help, but that they vill not see. The Seelie court the villain is not, but nonetheless against them they move. Blind and deaf their anger has them made, and into terrible error vill them lead."

"One small Fiederfolk I am, and to prevent a tragedy, this small thing I can do." she said as the ropes on Morgan's wrists parted beneath her knife.

"But there is more that you can do."

"A geas on you I do not lay." said Estelle, moving to cut the ropes on Morgan's ankles. "For your help, I only ask."

"Please. The lies that have been told expose, and the truth of who our enemies are reveal. The var between our peoples stop before it starts."

"and, if you can, please mein sister Ariella, back to me bring. A foolish girl" said the swan maid with a tear in her eye "but very dear to me she is."

There was a long silence again. Sam looked at Morgan. Morgan looked at Sam. An unspoken message passed between them, and then they both looked at Estelle once more.

"Well, what's a few more impossible tasks amongst new friends?" said Sam flippantly. "Someone's got to do it, and why not us? It certainly won't be the first time that we've been called upon to save the world on short notice."

"I'm with you." said Morgan. "That's a big job and we're just two ordinary people, but we'll do the best that we can, and just hope that it will be enough."

"Speak for yourself" said Sam, grandly. "There's nothing ordinary about this cat. I'm handsome and talented and smart; and an all-around triple threat. And I'm just about ready to kick some Unseelie butt, big – time."

Estelle laughed out loud. And the last strands of rope around Morgan's ankles fell away.

"Now if this vay you vill kindly step" she said "I think that out under the back canvas of the tent I can slip you."

Morgan stood, stretched out to regain the feeling in her feet, then followed the swan maiden, her faithful feline friend close behind her.

Thirty- Eight
Turned Away

The lands of enchantment lie side by side with our world, as close to our world as the two sides of a piece of paper. They're always there, but sometimes they're easier to see than others. The lands of enchantment are closer to ours in all of the places that lie between, that are neither one place or another. At crossroads and on stairs and at corners and all of the places that lie between. Some of them come and go from one place to another.

Sam and Morgan arrived just before the appointed time at the next place where the gates would open. They took shelter in the doorway of a store across the street, Morgan pretending to window shop as they watched for reality to change.

And it did. There was a rippling in reality. There was a slight shifting and suddenly a gate between two shops, where there was no "between" before. The space between the shops "opened up" revealing large wooden gates, carved with twining vines and birds and fantastic beasts, with mystic runes alight in the center. The gates were very obvious; yet no passersby seemed to notice them, or indeed that there was any "between" appearing at all.

Sam and Morgan crossed the street to the gates. Morgan took hold of the immense knocker and knocked briefly but firmly upon the massive structures. The knock boomed deeply and hollowly – echoing back, and back, and back, through long and empty rooms and hall ways.

They waited.

They waited for quite a while…

Sam looked at Morgan. Morgan looked at Sam. This was unusual. Usually, there was someone watching the gate at all times. Perhaps something was wrong. Morgan hesitantly tried the latch and found the gates firmly locked.

They waited some more.

Finally, they heard the sound of someone coming – coming from a long way away. The steps were slow and meticulous. They sounded tired. It took them time to progress gradually from the point where the woman and the golden cat could first hear them to the gate itself.

A peep hole opened in the great door, and an eye cautiously peered through. The peep hole slid shut again. The great oaken doors creaked open slowly, and Sam and Morgan found themselves facing a familiar but unexpected face. They had met the palm reader during their previous adventure but had not expected to see her here. The gate was usually tended by an official gate-keeper with a squadron of guards in support, not a single tired looking human.

She blinked at them, as if she hadn't seen the sun in some time. "Well, hello." said the palm reader "it's been awhile since we last saw each other. So, what can I do for you fine folks?

"Hel…lo?..." said Morgan, carefully. "We're here with an important message for the leaders of the Seelie court."

The palm reader sighed.

"I'm afraid, my dears." she said kindly "that there's a problem with that. We're having a small crisis here. A mystical plague of some sort is sweeping the Seelie court, and there's almost no one left standing to take your message, let alone do anything about it. I'd advise that you take a few steps further away so you don't catch anything from me and give your message to me to pass on, if you're comfortable with that."

Sam and Morgan took three steps back in unison. Morgan opened her mouth, and then paused. Sam had no such inhibitions.

"Some of the Unseelie have created a bit of a crisis themselves." the golden cat said. "They've butchered a wedge of swan warriors of the Mantelfiederfolk, kidnapped their princess, and left false evidence to indicate that the Seelie are the villains."

"Right now, a war band of Fiederfolk are on their way here to knock down these gates, rescue their princess and obtain the wergild for their fallen warriors in blood from the Seelie court. We've tried to tell them who really did this, but their leader would not believe us, and we only escaped because one of them had more sense than the rest."

"We came to warn the court so that it could prepare to defend itself." said Morgan. "You're telling us that the entire court is too sick to act?"

The palm reader looked at her sadly and nodded. "This came on fast and took them unawares." she said. "They had to call for outside healers like me, because all of their own went down with it too."

She wiped her brow with her kerchief.

"My husband and I have been working with no let - up for almost two days straight, just trying to get on top of it." she said exhaustedly. "I can tell that you hoped that getting here with the information would be enough and that this crisis could be turned over to someone else. Normally it would. I'm sorry that that's currently not so."

She smiled at them weakly. "As the present unofficial gate keeper, I thank you for telling us. The information is important and may give us time to make some preparations. I'll pass your message on inside to anyone still aware enough to hear it. Unfortunately, there's not much more that we can do at this point."

She looked at them for a long moment.

"You've done so much already" she said finally. "Unfortunately, I'm going to have to ask you to do even more. The court cannot do anything at this point, and yet something must surely be done. In its current state, the Mantelfiederfolk could surely destroy the court and leave themselves weakened in the process. They'd then be vulnerable to the villains that caused this entire situation. In addition, with the Seelie court gone, the physical world would suffer as well."

"The court should deal with threats of this type, but right now it cannot. We can't wait until they recover, for it'll be too late."

"Last fall, I saw you overcome odds that seemed insurmountable. I'm sorry but I'm going to have to ask you to do it again. There's no one else, so I have to ask you to keep going. Find the missing swan princess. Stop the Fiederfolk from attacking the Court. If you can, find proof of who's really responsible for these terrible deeds. Protect the court, and the world with it. Do what you can, and I will do what I can do as well."

"Are you willing?" she asked.

Morgan looked at Sam. Sam looked at Morgan. And then, they both looked back at her.

"Well, it was turning out to be a rather slow day." said Sam. "A little bit of saving the world again might be just what we need to liven things up."

He smiled. Morgan and the palm reader did too.

"Thank you" said the palm reader gratefully. "Is there anything that I can do for you?"

"Just lock the doors tightly, keep the hall as safe as you can, and get the Seelie on their feet as quickly as possible." said Morgan. "We make no promises, but we'll do the best that we can."

"If you need any information, just call us" said the palm reader, holding up a cell phone. "I know that you have our number and I believe the message will reach us even through the ether. Keep safe, my dears."

"And you as well." said Morgan, noting the look of exhaustion on her face. The palm reader smiled once more and closed the gate.

The cat and the woman stood and watched as the gate shimmered and disappeared, and the two shops moved back together once more.

Morgan looked down at Sam.

"What have we gotten ourselves into?" she asked rhetorically.

Sam looked back up at her.

"It was your idea to pull the blasted swan knight inside and off of the porch." he said.

Morgan blinked at him.

"My suggestion, on the other hand" the golden cat continued "is to plot, plan and regroup down the street at that coffee shop that I can see from here. They might just have sandwiches."

Thirty-Nine
Tea and Pendulums

After a quick stop in the stationary store next door, Morgan sat comfortably at a café table outside of the coffee shop, sipping tea and feeding small chunks of roast beef sandwich to her oversized shoulder bag.

"Office supplies, eh?" said Sam. "Not like there's a lot of space in here. If you're going to do this on a regular basis, you're going to have to invest in a larger purse."

Morgan smiled.

"Or a smaller cat." she thought, but she didn't say it. She was fond of her furry companion and wouldn't hurt his feelings for the world.

"So, find the princess and save the world" said the voice in her purse. "Sounds like a pretty typical day at our house. You got any ideas about how?"

"Sounds like dowsing again would be a good start." said Morgan uncertainly. "After that, we figure it out."

She reached down into her purse, and, rummaging carefully around the cat, came out with her pendulum and the tourist map. Spreading the map out, she set to work.

She asked the three classic questions again to start- "can I dowse?", "should I dowse?' and "may I dowse?" Each time the answer came back as a "yes".

"Can you show me where the swan princess is hidden?" Morgan asked the pendulum.

The pendulum went still. It momentarily quivered and then jerked. Finally, it began to swing in a very small "no" direction.

Morgan's heart filled with dismay. "No?" she said. "Sam, I think something's wrong here. When I asked the pendulum if it could tell me where the swan princess was, it acted funny, and then told me no."

159

She had an awful thought.

"Is the swan princess still alive?" she asked the pendulum, afraid of the answer.

It began to swing in the "yes" direction.

Morgan let out a deep breath she hadn't realized she was holding. "She's alive, Sam" she told the cat "but when I asked the pendulum if it could tell me where she was, it said no."

"Well, with two days experience, you're still the dowsing expert of the two of us." said the cat from inside of her purse. "Can you think of anything that would explain why the pendulum is acting that way? Or any way to get answers that help us?"

Morgan closed her eyes and cast her mind back to her first lesson in using a pendulum. It took a moment, but then the memory of the tarot reader's voice echoed in her head. "At some times, the pendulum may start to act oddly." he said. "It may stop dead, or rapidly swing alternately yes and no, or wobble all over the place. When it does this, it usually means you've asked a question that can't be answered with a clear "yes" or "no"."

"For instance," said the tarot reader, "say I had an offer of a job that would bring me a lot of money but make me absolutely crazy. If I asked the pendulum if this would be a good job for me, it might have a hard time answering clearly yes or no. Giving you an odd response is the way the pendulum tells you that you need to ask in a different way. With the job offer example, asking "Will I make a lot of money in this job?", "Will I be happy in this job?" or "Is there a better job offer for me that I should be looking for instead?" gives me a clearer picture of the entire situation."

"Remember," he said "if the pendulum starts acting oddly, it's usually time to adjust the question."

Morgan re-opened her eyes and refocused on the

question that faced her now. "Sam" she said. "I think the odd answer means the pendulum can't answer the question the way I asked it."

"So, let's start from there." said Sam. "What exactly did you ask?"

Morgan thought carefully, in order to get the exact words as closely as possible. "I asked "Can you show me where the swan princess is hidden?" she said. "And the pendulum started doing odd things, wobbling and twisting and ending up with giving me a very tiny "no"

There was a thoughtful silence from her purse. The sound of feline brains at work.

"Sounds like there may be something getting in the way of dowsing for her." he said finally. "Now we know that you can dowse to find people, especially the swan people. That's how we found the camp even though it was moving. Is it possible there's something interfering with you dowsing for this particular swan princess?"

Morgan held up the pendulum, positioning it so it could swing freely from her hand at will. "Is there something interfering to finding the swan princess by dowsing?" she asked.

The pendulum began to swing vigorously, the size of the swing indicating a definite "yes!"

"Is it something that I know about?" asked Morgan/

The pendulum gave her an emphatic "yes!" once more.

"Something I've been told about?" she asked.

"Yes." came back the answer.

"Is it a spell?" inquired Sam.

"Is it a spell?" repeated Morgan.

The pendulum started wobbling again. Answer not clear, so question is problematic.

"Not really a spell then. Hmm." said Morgan, trying

to think of other options.

She paused for a moment, trying to think of other questions to narrow things down. The tarot reader had told her that sometimes the hardest part of working with a pendulum was asking the right question.

"Something that I've had personal experience of?" she finally asked in desperation, reaching for options.

The pendulum paused, and then began to swing in the "yes" direction again.

Morgan was floored. She'd asked that because she couldn't think of anything else. It seemed this was a step in the right direction.

"Sam" she said excitedly "the pendulum says that I have personal experience that explains why we can't find the swan princess by dowsing. I only learned the basics of dowsing yesterday. What kind of experience could I have that could apply here?"

'Well, first, we should rule out what you know about dowsing." said Sam.

Morgan looked at the pendulum. "Is this experience part of what I've learned about dowsing? she asked.

The pendulum indicated a small, unhappy "no".

"No" she relayed to Sam. "What could it be?"

"Well, you've been learning about metaphysics" said the cat. "Let's start at the beginning. Is it something you experienced during our previous adventure last fall?"

"Is it something I experienced during the last time I was on the run from the Unseelie?" asked Morgan.

A firm "yes" from the pendulum.

"Was it something that I experienced during the quest while Sam was with me?" she asked.

"No" to that.

"Something that I experienced while Sam and I were separated?" asked Morgan.

The pendulum moved in the yes direction.

"Well, I can't help you with that then" said Sam. "You've told me some of what happened while you were on your own, but I don't remember anything about dowsing or being unable to find things."

Being unable to find things.

Morgan closed her eyes, and let her mind reach gently out. Something she could almost remember about finding people and concealing people was niggling at the edge of her mind. If she mentally snuck upon it, she might be able to catch hold of that memory before it was startled and ran away.

Suddenly her mind was back there, back at the Renaissance faire she'd fled to last fall. That was when she first started to learn about the magick that filled the world around her, when Sam had first revealed himself to be her guardian.

Back then, the change in rulers of the sidhe court had put Sam and herself on a desperate race to reach the court itself before Unseelie hunters could find her and stop her permanently. At one point, they'd been separated when Sam stayed behind to slow those pursuing her. At a loss to find her destination now that her feline guide was amongst the missing, she'd fallen back on the only other option she could think of- contacting the tarot reader who was working at the renaissance faire. He and the palm reader had hidden her from the Unseelie hunters pursuing her and helped on her way.

"There was something there," thought Morgan in frustration. "Something about hiding people."

And then, she had it.

"Won't they find me out in the open like that?" Morgan heard her own voice asking.

"If they're tracking you by magick or by your energy

field, our tent is one of the best places you could be, because our personal energy fields and our wards should mask your energy from them." she remembered the palm reader telling her.

She remembered how the two readers had concealed her from her pursuers by boosting the levels of their own energy fields, concealing her energy behind theirs. She also remembered how the palm reader had further muddled the issue for the Unseelie sidhe by sending out a number of her other friends with energy fields to wander the faire. They'd walked in pairs of women, laying false traces for the hunters, while the palmist and Morgan had strolled to the front gate arm in arm, with Morgan's energy concealed by hers.

Morgan suddenly had new ideas about why she couldn't dowse for the swan princess. "The reason I can't dowse for the swan princess – is it because an energy field can be concealed by a stronger one?" she asked the pendulum.

The pendulum almost leaped out of her hand, with an emphatic "Yes!"

"The reason I can't find the swan princess by dowsing is that her energy field is hidden behind another one stronger than hers?" continued Morgan.

The pendulum indicated "yes" again.

"Think that you're really onto something there." said Sam. Morgan thought so, too. She stopped and thought for a moment about this.

"Can I dowse for areas of high metaphysical energy?" she asked. Once more, the answer from the pendulum was "yes".

"Batting a thousand there." said Sam. "What's your next question?"

"Can I narrow down possible locations of the princess by identifying areas of high energy that might hide her energy field?" Morgan asked the pendulum. The answer once again was "yes".

"Good call, Morgan" said Sam "Now I think that you'd better get busy nailing down those areas for us. We've got a lot of ground to cover and not much time."

Morgan smiled, and went back to work with her pendulum and the map

Forty
Storming the Gates

It was nearing midday when the Mantelfiederfolk arrived at the place where the gates to the Seelie court were next due to appear. The swan folk rode bold and brassily, all furs and feathers and obscure weapons, mounted on massive horses heavily draped in resplendent barding. There was nothing reserved about the Fiederfolk going to war, but, just as Claud the swan knight had once said, they had the ability to pass unnoticed in the waking world if they chose, as loud and as outrageous as they might be. Pedestrians strolled by, cars drove down the street, joggers jogged and dogs were walked but no one seemed to notice the handsome group of Germanic barbarians.

Hildreth was in a bad mood. Her warriors had been slaughtered, her eldest daughter kidnapped and possibly dead, her prisoners had told her a fanciful tale and then escaped from her keeping, and her instincts were beginning to whisper that there was something here that she was missing. The look on the face of the leader of her warriors was not helping either. She knew that look. It was the look that he got when there was something he thought was important to tell her, but was afraid that she would not want to hear it.

Hildreth grunted quietly to herself. A certain amount of respect, awe and even fear was appropriate in a subordinate, and she felt good that she commanded that from her followers. Still, if it was important, being in a position of responsibility, he owed it to her to tell her, even if she became angry about it. The way things were going, she just might have to kick the information out of him.

Yet still, she thought philosophically, still she was at war. Things could be far worse.

The gate was due to open at this particular place in twelve hours. As far as Hildreth was concerned, this would not do. They would just have to operate on S.C.T. (Swan Central Time.)

Hildreth dismounted and faced the space where the gates would appear. Her warriors dismounted as well and formed up in a wedge, backing her position.

The shaman of the swan people closed her eyes and concentrated for just a moment, focusing on the energy that she was about to move to shift reality and the task that she was going to put it to. When her focus was clear in her mind, her eyes opened.

Chanting, Hildreth unsheathed her long knife and drew it across her palm in one smooth stroke. Blood welled from the wound that she had just dealt herself.

She wiped her knife emphatically across her thigh, cleaning it and sheathing it, and then focused herself to work.

Drawing the symbol in her head. Drawing the symbol in the air with her blooded hand. Using her chant to push energy that she was raising through concentration and sacrifice to serve her purpose.

She concentrated. She caught hold of something that no physical force could grasp.

And, slowly, painfully, a narrow tunnel leading to the gates to the Seelie court came into view, long before it was supposed to.

Hildreth drew out her long knife from out of its sheath once more. With a final shout and the full force of her will, she drove the knife firmly into the earth, locking knife into the ground and gate with it into the physical world.

Working complete, she stopped then and bent over, hands on her knees, breathing deeply and trying to keep from vomiting. A leader should never be seen losing control, and that included control of her stomach

The gate strained at the bindings of her magick, but they were locked firmly in place by the sheer force of her will. They gradually resigned themselves to captivity.

After a moment of deep breathing, re-centering and not vomiting, Hildreth regained herself once more. She stood upright and strode across the green to the gates to the Seelie court.

She raised a massive fist and knocked like thunder upon the door.

ONCE she knocked – and the impact boomed and rolled through the empty halls.

TWICE she knocked – and the blow echoed, meeting the first blow and multiplying.

THRICE she knocked – and the halls filled with a monstrous sound, rattling the walls and shaking the foundations.

Hildreth took a single step back and looked up at the distant tops of the gates that were facing her and the massive structures beyond them.

"COME OUT!" she bellowed at the gates and at those who lay behind them. "COME OUT! COME OUT!"

"Mein people, you have killed! Mein daughter, you have taken! Upon the Mantelfiederfolk, the People of the Cloak of Feathers, var you have declared– and a decision this is that sorely regret you vill!"

"Your surrender, ve demand! Satisfaction, ve demand! A verguild, a blood price for those who have passed beyond the veil of Death, ve demand! "

And the return of mein Ariella, mein daughter, be she living or dead, ve demand. Anyone who a finger on her has laid vill that day rue!"

She moved closer to the gate again and once more began to pound upon it.

"COME OUT!" she cried
"COME OUT!"
"COME OUT!"
And the gate began to slowly bend and to give way
beneath the sheer power of her blows

Forty-One
Finding the Sorcerer's Lair

They'd followed the guidance of pendulum and map from one patch of high energy to another, eliminating places that did not conceal the princess and having some fairly alarming experiences along the way. They'd found a curious bracelet lying in the mud near horse tracks. Sam sniffed it gingerly and said it smelled like swan, so they were finally in the right area. Now they were lying on their stomachs behind some shrubbery, looking down at a surge of Unseelie activity below.

"Well, I've had fun, and that was certainly not it." said Sam. "Who would have thought that there were so many dangerous pockets of magick that could hide a swan princess scattered throughout this town? The bracelet says we're in the right area but I'm hoping that we've found the right site at last."

Morgan nodded quietly. She was hoping so, too.

They lay on their stomachs in the grass, hidden from the activity in the dell below. They watched as Unseelie warriors emerged from a rough stone tunnel in the earth and could only be glad that the dark hunds seemed to currently have business elsewhere.

Two warriors reined in flame eyed horses, just below where they laid concealed.

"Still thinking about that little swan princess, are you not?" said the first.

His companion glared at him.

"You are lucky that you listened to me and kept your hands off of her." continued the first warrior." You knew that she was to be delivered here to the sorcerer, and he does not like it when the rank and file play with his things. He would have had your head at the very least if we had not made his "delivery" intact."

The second Unseelie warrior glared again, and kicked his horse into movement.

Sam looked at Morgan. Morgan looked at Sam. It seemed they had at last found the place where the swan princess was being kept hidden. Evidently, she had only arrived shortly before them, and might therefore still be alive.

Now all that they had to do was figure out how to make their way past a mass of Unseelie warriors and an evil sorcerer.

Forty- Two
In the Sick Rooms

It had been a long night and a long day and another besides in the sick rooms of the Seelie and there were few signs that things were going to get better soon. Most of the members of the court were flat on their backs with the plague, so weak that they could barely lift their heads. They all needed healing and tending, and there were too few capable of doing that or even taking care of themselves.

The palmist was beginning to feel the strain. She and her partner, the tarot reader, had been on the job for over two days now, healing the sick, tending them, and organizing any others not yet too sick to stand.

She was feeling the energy of the sick room as well. Not just the heavy energy of multiple beings exhausted and ill, but also the fell energy of the magick at the root of the plague. The tarot reader had quietly told her what he had found (and what he had not) during his journeywork, but even before he had looked for it, she had felt the effect of uncanny influences. She had known that this plague would have to be fought on multiple levels.

And, if that were not enough, now they had the threat of incoming swan people, ready for war. The day just kept getting better and better.

The eldritch energy wore at her as much as the physical labor did. It surged and receded, never leaving her a handle to get a hold of it. At points, it seemed to beat on her defenses, making her dizzy. She could feel it in her bones, pounding and pounding.

A cloud of pixies fluttered in, airlifting in more cloths to soak in cold water and apply to fevered brows. A wooden bucket of cold water soon followed, carried by a sturdy little faun who was beginning to look a little woozy himself. The bucket clunked as he dropped it to the floor, overflowing slightly.

The palmist sighed as she pulled herself out of the chair she had sat in for a minute. She crossed to the bucket and dropped a cloth into it, soaking it thoroughly as she carried bucket and cloths to the next bed in the great hall. An impromptu mass infirmary had been set up here to make it easier for the few healers still on their feet to tend the sick efficiently and keep them under observation.

Down one side and up the other. Up and down endless aisles of beds, checking for fevers, applying damp cloths to clammy foreheads, lifting heads to get parched throats to drink, carefully portioning out such healing energy as she still had to the worst cases and keeping a close eye on which cases were headed downhill.

Across the hall, she could see her beloved partner, the tarot reader, in the distance moving slowly down the aisles on that side of the room, also watching, healing and tending. The sight of him gave her energy and hope, but still the rows of sick and exhausted creatures seemed to go on forever and there seemed to be no end to it.

She was beginning to feel tired and even a bit discouraged.

No. Just no, she chided herself internally. They'd get through this. They always got through whatever happened. The citizens of the Seelie court would heal at last, the situation with the swan folk would be resolved and life would go on again. It always did.

She'd best get back to work again to make sure that that happened

She took a deep breath and threw her shoulders back before bending to work once more. Back to her duty now. Feeling foreheads, mopping brows, pushing fluids to face after face after face. Trickle-feeding energy where it would do the most good. Rinse and repeat and rinse and repeat again. Keeping going at the job in front of her as best she could.

Sit for a moment and breathe in the energy of the earth. Soles of her feet flat against the ground and breathing up energy from the earth's core- energy that was always there for her. She could breathe in the energy and pass it on to her patients to support their healing, but her own body was tiring. There was only so much that the energy that she was breathing into her body and resting could do. She was tiring, and soon enough would have to stop to rest and to recover her own center.

There was a pounding in her head. Perhaps she was reaching her limits. The palmist shook her head and the pounding receded into the distance. It almost sounded like a booming sound coming from somewhere, like the sound of knocking, though it could also have been some grandiose elven alarm clock or a Seelie shutter flapping in an unearthly breeze. Someone knocking at a door. Someone actually wanted into a place that she wanted out of- a place that any sane person would surely avoid like the plague.

That's crazy. They were crazy, whoever they were, and she'd be crazy if she took a break from this marathon healing event to go check the door to see if there was actually someone out there.

The palmist sighed. She had not slept in for two nights now. Perhaps hallucinations were setting in.

The distant knocking sound continued.

The palmist swiped away a tendril of hair that had escaped her head cloth and was trailing down the side of her face again, tickling the corner of her eye.

"Kitten," she said tiredly "It sounds like there's someone knocking at the gates. Can you possibly go and find out who it is out there? And then please just ask if they could possibly come back at some other time? Any other time? Please? Because my schedule's just about full up for now." she added, brushing that annoying little hair out of the way again.

The winged kitten had been helping by running messages and hovering in the air to watch the patients for any signs of worsening illness. The help that he gave was limited, but he was decorative while doing it. Only four months and a bit old, he was doing pretty well for someone in his age group. The palmist would take any help that she could get at this point and be glad of it.

The kitten licked his paw and contemplated her for a minute. "Yesssss… Yesss. I can do dat" he announced at last. "I will check de door for any knocker type folks and will get back to you de quickest, right?

Even exhausted, the palmist had to smile at the tiny bundle of self-importance "Get back to me de quickest- yes." she agreed nodding. "and thank you very much."

"You to be welcome" the winged kitten said. He took to the air, fluttering out and down the hall.

The palmist smiled, and then turned back to her next patient, face serious once more. With all of the sick people to tend and the shortage of other helpers, she didn't have a spare moment to think about anything else.

That was a problem. A big problem.

It didn't occur to her that the gates should not be in contact with the earth at this time and that there was no way that someone could be knocking at them.

No way on earth.

Forty-Three
At the Gates

The winged kitten fluttered out of the great hall and down through an assortment of halls and rooms, making his way towards the far away gates. Under normal conditions, the gates rotated in and out of phase with the world of humans, and there were only certain times when they would be open in that world. The gates also rotated through space as well as time so the gates wouldn't always appear in the same place. The rotation of the gates made the Seelie court accessible from the human world by those who knew the time and place that the gates would appear, but did not leave the court too accessible to those who had no business visiting. This was a defense for both the members of the court and the court itself.

For this reason, Hildreth's magick was extraordinary. Through blood and chant and force of will alone, she had wrested control of the gates for now from the one who had originally cast the spell on them. That was both dangerous and unprecedented in the history of the elven courts.

If the kitten had been a bit older, if the kitten had had a bit more experienced, he would have known that there was something wrong here. He would have known that nothing could possibly have been knocking on the front gates now because nothing could have possibly reached them from the outside. He would have certainly been warier in approaching the gate.

Lacking experience, wariness and knowledge of the normal schedule of the gates, the kitten thought nothing of the knocking that grew louder as he flew closer to the outer gates. He fluttered along, very pleased with himself and very proud that he was able to help the humans in such grown up ways.

He was a big kitty now. They needed a really big kitty just like him. They needed the winged kitten. And they were very, very lucky to have him at this exciting time in the history of the elven court.

The noise at the gate grew louder as he made his way through winding halls and many rooms to reach it. There definitely was someone knocking at the outer gates to the court. That began to make him uneasy.

The winged kitten was too young and inexperienced to know the gate should not be accessible now, but he had an impression that something was just not right. He couldn't quite put his paw on it, but he had an uncomfortable feeling there was something going on that he was missing.

His nose wrinkled just a little bit. He was thinking very hard, trying to figure it all out. And, as he thought, he flew closer to the gates and to the sound of the knocking.

The knocking was louder now as he got close to the gate, and he began to hear sounds that sounded like someone yelling. Someone was shouting angrily outside of the gates and pounding hard, too hard on them

The kitten stopped short and hovered in place for a moment. He was a very brave kitten but this was becoming a tiny bit scary, as very brave a kitty as he was. He might not know exactly when the gates were normally accessible, but he did at least know that, when people came to visit the court, they usually didn't come banging and demanding and shouting loudly. That was not the way that people usually behaved at court – or if they did act that way, they didn't usually get to stay there for long.

When people sought audience at court, they were usually polite and respectful, because the Seelie court contained some of the most frightening beings and creatures around. At that point, courtesy was both polite and a survival trait. It not only made you more likely to get in the gates, but also made you more likely to survive and to possibly even come away with what you had come for.

He thought, and thought hard. The sound was scary, that was true, and something was just not right about the way things were happening. Still, he was a very brave kitten and had been sent on an important mission. Since so many Seelie citizens were down with the plague, each one of them must do the best that he could.

He did the winged kitten equivalent of a shrug (which would have been interesting to see, if anyone had been on their feet and present to see it.) Whatever happened, he would deal with it, because he was a smart and fierce and brave winged kitten.

And winged kittens rule.

The kitten darted straight forwards through the air once again, headed straight towards the loudly echoing front gates.

Hildreth's fist pounded on the door. The sound of the blows echoed like thunder

"COME OUT!" she cried

"COME OUT!"

"COME OUT!"

The wood and the metal of the gate groaned and cried out beneath her knocking. She was knocking not only with her fist but also with her magic. The force of her blows left deep dents in the wood of the massive gates. She was knocking with all of her power. She was knocking with all of her rage. She was knocking with a force enormous and inhuman.

And no one came in answer to her knocking. No one at all.

It was an enormous insult. An insult to her. An insult to her people. It was not enough that they had slaughtered her people. It was not enough that they had abducted her eldest daughter. Beyond all of that, they had so little respect for her and her people that they could not even be bothered to answer the door when she and her warriors came in full martial array.

She would have to teach them some respect for the Mantelfiederfolk. She would teach them what an angry swan warrior was capable of, and she would also show them what an entire war band of swan warriors could do.

She pounded harder on the oaken gates, her face flushing deep red with her anger and the veins sticking out in her neck.

"COME OUT!" she cried loudly

"COME OUT!"

"COME OUT!"

The wood began to crumple slightly under the force of her blows and the metal of the hinges began to strain.

"COME OUT!" she cried loudly.

"COME OUT!"

"COME OUT!"

And suddenly, without any warning, a little window opened in the gates at face level.

Hildreth had been knocking for a long time. She had decided that she was being deliberately snubbed by the Seelie court, and that she would have to make them listen to her by force. At this point she was no longer expecting anyone to answer the door and was therefore startled by the little window opening.

Taken by surprise, she froze with her fist in midair, half way to knocking again. Caught in this position, she felt a little foolish. She brought her clenched fist down once more to her side.

She raised her glance from the wood that she had been knocking on to the window itself and was surprised once again

Peering out at her from the opened spy window was a tiny grey face; a fuzzy, furry, face; a little face that might just possibly be called darling if you were not a fierce and savage swan warrior and shaman.

"Hal-lo" said the kitten, lisping ever so slightly. "Wel-come to de Seelie court. We bids yu wel-come, here at de court."

This was unbelievable. First, they have so little respect for her and the Mantelfiederfolk that they do not answer the door when she had caught it out of time and space and wrenched it under her control, and then, then, when they finally did respond, they sent someone as small and insignificant as this to treat with her. It was an insult. It was an insult of monstrous proportions.

"What be yur buzness wid de court of de Seelie king?" asked the kitten. "Because I haf been sent to find out who is to be out here at de gate and take a message for later."

That was an even bigger insult. They could not even be bothered to treat with her now. It was an enormous insult and could not be tolerated.

The kitten cocked his head slightly to the one side and waited for her response with deep interest. Her face was turning all different, interesting colors now and the vein in her temple was beginning to pulse slightly. He had never seen anything as fascinating as this before in all of his young life

Indignation and rage warred in the swan shaman's head to the point that she could not even get a word out for a minute. What a great insult this was! That one great power should receive an official declaration of war from another great power by sending such an insignificant emissary with such a total lack of any respect or diplomatic skills of any kind.

Could he for later a message take? **Could he for later a message take?**

She would give him a message for later all right- and the words began to flow in full plenty where but a moment ago she was speechless.

The winged kitten listened interestedly at first but his interest soon turned into alarm. He was not old enough to understand everything the big angry lady with the feathery cloak was saying to him, but he was catching a word here and a word there and some of the words that he was catching were **just not nice words!**

It was an insult. It was an insult of monstrous proportions.

He was surely a helpful kitten, yes, but he was also a cat and cats just did not have to put up with this kind of disrespect. Still, he was on the job, and no one would be able to say that his manners fell short in any way.

"Tank you for calling," the winged kitten lisped, breaking through the torrent of abuse streaming out of the swan shaman. "and tank you for bringing yur concerns to de Seelie court. I will take yur message and tell de officials uv de court dat yu haf called so dat dey can get back to you at a more convenient time for you an dem both."

"an I wish to yu a very nice day" he added and swung the door to the window shut with one velvet paw.

"Whew" the winged kitten thought "dat was awful. Still" he brightened "I did o.k. at dis. I had better get back and tell de nice healer all about who is to be knocking."

And he fluttered back into the depths of the palace again.

Hildreth stared at the door in total disbelief.

They had ignored her! They had sent a minor minion to meet with her! They had told her that they had no time for her now! And then they had cut her off in midsentence!

If she had thought she was as enraged as she could be come before, she knew different now.

They had no respect. No respect at all. And she was going to have to teach them some.

Now.

Beyond the oaken gates to the Seelie court, a roar of inarticulate rage went up, and the pounding on the front gates started again more frantically than before. The metal hinges of the door began to creak.

Forty-Four
Ariella Loosens Her Bonds

The swan princess lay on the stony ground, bound and gagged but mind active, even if her body could not be. She quietly strained at her bonds, testing them from every angle, looking for the edge that would let her escape.

In the meantime, the sorcerer continued to clear the central table, talking constantly.

"Talk, talk, talk..." Ariella thought distractedly. "their next plot over the vorld to take or their evil vills upon people to vork. Is that all that evil villains about think? Vith these guys anyway, vat it is? Some better hobbies they need."

And the ropes binding her hands began to slip.

She found some slack in the rope and worked at it, gradually gaining more play in the bonds. Circulation slowly began to return to her wrists and fingers. The ropes had been drawn cruelly tight and she was now experiencing a collection of pins and needles. She wriggled her hands, trying desperately to regain control. She strained with her ankles, trying to gain similar results for her feet.

She could feel her hands again and was beginning to feel some give at her feet, when the sorcerer finished his preparations and turned to her at last.

"All ready, my dear" he smiled evilly. "And now it is time to introduce you into the equation."

He bent down and slid his arms under her at knees and shoulders. With a grunt, he lifted her off of the floor, boosting her in his arms to get a better grip upon her.

She leaned into him, hiding the sight of loosening ropes.

He turned and carried her across the room to the table. He was tall and cadaverous, but strong, his muscles like whip cord and iron. He lifted her body onto the table, depositing her with some accuracy but scant ceremony.

She lay there, looking up at him. Her hands were partially free, but her feet still restrained and lacked feeling. She was likely to fall if she tried to stand, let alone walk or run.

"Now you just lie there and rest, my dear" the sorcerer said. "The stars are not quite in alignment yet– but they will be soon. Very soon. And then we both shall see what I can accomplish with the power of the moon and the swan in your blood to support me."

"Don't scream" she thought wildly. "Don't scream."

The sorcerer turned away from her.

And Ariella continued to quietly work at her bonds.

Forty-Five
Winging It

In most epic stories, the heroes have a brilliant plan to storm the castle, steal the MacGuffin or rescue the princess. They have cunning plans, devious plots, tricky apparatuses or loyal followers who will risk all to achieve the ultimate goals and save the day.

It would have been nice to have a brilliant plan. It would have been great to have a cunning plan, a devious plot, a tricky apparatus or an adherent willing to risk all. Failing that, Morgan and Sam just had to improvise.

They didn't have much time. The longer they lurked outside of the sorcerer's lair, the more likely they were to be discovered. As they tried to figure out a cunning plan, the swan princess might be undergoing frightful tortures or even being killed.

They didn't have much time. The swan army was on the march and the Seelie court was powerless before them.

They didn't have much time for a brilliant plan; so they had to act without one.

They watched the comings and goings of the Unseelie warriors to get a feel for their routine. They looked at the land, looking for places to hide, vantage points and points of vulnerability. They took a quick inventory of what they had to work with.

And then they moved.

Cats evidently have the same ability as the Fiederfolk to move unseen if they choose. That's why you so often find cats in places they couldn't possibly have gotten into.

Sam flattened himself to the ground and edged across the terrain from cover to cover, making his way down into the dell and as close to the opening in the hillside as possible.

Meanwhile, Morgan was gathering small stones for

a time-honored tradition. She waited until Sam was in position, and then waited some more until the next group of warriors came out of the tunnel. Quickly, she tossed a stone overhand, so it landed on the opposite side of the clearing, far from herself and Sam. It caused an audible rustle in the thick bushes.

The Unseelie warriors, relaxed a moment ago, targeted immediately on the noise. Their heads snapped around and their eyes locked on where the leaves rustled.

Morgan froze. She was glad there were no dark hunds here on patrol.

Sam took his chance and slipped quickly into the tunnel, moving like smoke. He disappeared swiftly into the darkness.

The warriors scanned the area, eyes and ears focused keenly all around them, looking for intruders. Morgan held her breath, trying to avoid attracting any attention.

The warriors looked. The warriors listened. And, gradually, as nothing hostile presented itself to them, they began to relax again.

And, when they relaxed, Morgan threw the second rock to another area, far from herself and the tunnel mouth.

The warriors tensed again. They oriented onto the sound like hunting dogs pointing at a game bird. They looked and they listened.

Morgan froze, just as before. While she didn't have the power to pass unseen in the waking world, (like some folks she could think of) she was getting pretty good at this "hold–your–breath–in–raw-terror–lest–you- give-yourself– away" kind of thing.

"Better take a look and see if something suspicious is going on." muttered one of the Unseelie. "Himself will certainly, get his mystical knickers in a twist if some foolish heroic do–gooder comes along and spoils his nasty magickal experiments. You and you, spread out and start checking the bushes."

"And who died and made you the king of the fairies?" asked another of the sidhe aggressively. "I do not seem to remember anyone raising you up to the level of command, boy-o."

"Oh, that is right" said the first warrior sarcastically. "That is right. You just keep thinking that, my friend. If some over–the–top Germanic swan knight comes swanning along and escapes with the princess that the sorcerer is so eager to be working with, you just go ahead and tell the boss you did not stop him because no one told you that I could tell you anything about how to defend the sorcerer's lair."

"He will like that. He will like that a lot."

There was a long silence while the second warrior thought that through to its logical and lethal conclusion. Most evil sorcerers don't like to have their fun spoiled.

"Well, right–oh, then!" he said finally. "I will just go this way and you go that way and we will all look for intruders, shall we?"

The first sidhe stifled something that could well have been a laugh in some other circumstances; and the Unseelie warriors all moved off in a group heading in the other direction.

Morgan blinked, a bit confused. Maybe the old tricks were the best ones after all.

Meanwhile, in the tunnel, Sam was moving rapidly and unseen. Now, cats can't go invisible, per se. But they can pass unnoticed. And Sam was as far beyond an average cat as a hot fudge ice cream sundae is beyond a snow cone.

There was no cover in the tunnel. Sam was hiding behind that lack of cover, making his way deeper and deeper into the underground headquarters.

Just as the Unseelie had done, Sam looked. Sam

listened. Unlike the warriors, Sam made good use of all his eyes and ears took in.

He passed barracks and mess areas. He passed kitchens and guard rooms. He passed rooms he preferred not to know the nature of.

And, at last, at long last, he came to a door to a room redolent with the aroma of magick and of swan.

Sam paused there. Carefully, cautiously, he listened at the oaken door.

Forty-Six
Rescue

The sorcerer was bent over another table, consulting a massive tome and fiddling with some arcane tool that Ariella really did not want to know more about. She struggled with her bonds. Soon, he had said. The moon would be right and he would turn to her for some arcane ritual he thought would give him the power of shape changing and flight, at the cost of her life.

Ariella knew that it wouldn't work. The sorcerer did not know as much as he thought about the mystical nature of her people, but his experiment would leave her unable to appreciate his frustration.

She wrenched again at her bonds, almost careless in an emotion that, in a lesser being than a Fiederfolk, might almost have passed for panic. She had to get loose! She had to get loose!

No one was going to find her in time. It was up to her to survive.

She stretched and tore at her bonds. She almost thrashed about on the table, trying to free her legs. And, caught up in her efforts, she missed the door opening, just a tiny crack.

The sorcerer noticed that she was not lying quietly awaiting her fate.

"Lively are you, eh?" he said, rising and striding over to the table on which she lay. "That's good, my girl. That is the vigor of the swan in your blood, the sheer force of life that soon shall be spilt in order to make me all the more powerful!"

He caught her face in his hand and squeezed it hard. Ariella froze for a moment from the pain.

"Go ahead, my dear" he sneered. "Struggle. Struggle

some more. Wake up that sweet swan dreaming in your blood. It will only make it more powerful when it comes at last to me!"

He bent over her. She began to flail at him as wildly as her bonds would permit. She thrashed about. She rocked from side to side. She glared at him with furious eyes and thrust her head forcefully towards him.

The sorcerer recoiled, intimidated by her anger. Then he smiled and bent towards her once more. Both of them were so focused on her struggles that neither noticed that there was someone else in the room.

The sorcerer raised a sharp and dangerous looking mystic tool, covered with cryptic symbols and edged with dark energy. He brandished it for effect before the eyes of the horrified swan princess. He smiled evilly.

And, then, with a yowl and a hiss, Sam attacked.

Sam leapt from the floor, yowling like a banshee. He struck with dagger-like claws at the sorcerer's hand, slicing him and making him drop the ominous blade with a curse. He lunged into the sorcerer's face, striking out with tooth and claw.

The sorcerer cried out. He swore. He raised his hands to protect his face and fell back in fear. This was not what he had been expecting to do with his day.

The sudden onset of sound and fury surprised Ariella, but she knew this was the chance she needed. She wrenched with all of her strength at the ropes on her hands, and at last they parted. She sat up forcibly, knocking the beset sorcerer aside and reaching for the ropes on her ankles. She strained with her legs and the ropes snapped.

She turned to drop her legs over the side of the table. The circulation returned to her legs with a rush and she cried out in pain, before biting her lip. Fiederfolk do not cry out in pain. They're strong. They do not weep.

The sorcerer was clutching at his wounds, dodging and dashing, cursing and swearing. Sam made little dashes at his ankles, striking deep into the tendons with every pass. The sorcerer tried to cast a spell or curse, but each time he started, the next stabbing pain broke his concentration.

Gathering herself together, Ariella slid off the marble table. She stood and almost fell again, feet still numb. She pulled herself to her feet once more by sheer force of Germanic will.

She staggered and took one step, and then another. She began to feel her feet again, and, although the pain was beyond severe, she still welcomed the returning feeling.

She looked around her for a weapon.

Sam made another pass at the lower half of the evil sorcerer (who was beginning to seriously wish that he had gone into a totally different line of work.) He struck deeply, cutting in with fang and claw, and then firmly caught hold of the now ragged hem of the sorcerer's robe. His feet left the ground as he worked his way upwards.

Up past the knees.

Up past the crotch, with a distracting lashing out which seriously fouled the sorcerer's concentration yet again.

Up past the sorcerers' chest, neatly evading flailing hands and resulting in the sorcerer hitting himself hard.

Up to the face.

And then Sam really began to go to work….

Outside of the sorcerer's lair, Morgan carefully kept watch as the warriors thrashed around in the distance, searching for the cause of the noise. She nervously clutched her small collection of stones, awaiting the soldiers' return and the need to distract them once more.

"I wonder what Sam's up to" she wondered nervously. "He's been in there for a long time. Hope he's ok."

She strained to hear the soldiers in the distance.

Back in the cavern, Sam was going wild. He'd been disguised as a kindly, calm, protective guardian cat for a very long time, but, at heart, he was still a tom cat and he hadn't had any outlet for that for a long time.

Now it was time to cut loose and get busy.

He was loving this.

Ariella leaned against the table, wide eyed.

"Vat the heck this is?' she thought. "In all my life, something like this I have never seen! Is this a spell wrong gone? A familiar spirit loose broke?"

She pulled herself together.

"Vatever it is" she thought "it is giving me the opening I need to possibly escape. The enemy of my enemy not always my friend is, but this creature, the sorcerer he is distracting. The edge I need, this may be."

"Help him I should." she thought. "Help him to kick this sorcerer's butt I should. If out it turns that friend to me he is not, also prepared to kick his butt I should be. Now, as a weapon, what can I use?"

Sam was making real progress here. The sorcerer was screaming, and bleeding, and crying, and thrashing about, unable to get a grip upon Sam no matter how much he tried. Sam had not enjoyed himself this much for years.

"Surrender!" he hissed in the ear he was chewing on. "Surrender or I will make your death such a hell that you will take nine deaths in the dying of it."

The sorcerer froze, panicked, and then struggled to get away.

And Sam continued to attack him.

Outside, Morgan was still hiding and listening. She felt very exposed with only the brush to conceal her.

She could hear the soldiers thrashing around in the brush. Searching seemed to be keeping them busy for now, but how long would that hold them? And what if another patrol returned to the cavern?

Frightened, Morgan still held her position. If the warriors returned, Sam was counting on her to keep them occupied and distracted, and the only way this "not–a–brilliant–plan" would work was if both of them were brave, reliable and played their parts.

She was frightened, but she held her ground.

Ariella would have been frightened, if her people ever became frightened. Fortunately, the Fiederfolk do not understand being frightened at all, so she didn't have that to deal with.

She quickly looked around with the eye of a warrior for any weapon she could use to join the fray. The pointed tool the sorcerer had been holding she mentally discarded at once. As a member of a warrior tribe, she had an automatic distrust of the trappings of magick other than the magick of her own people. (Besides, she had an uneasy feeling that an item an evil sorcerer was using with such enjoyment was something probably better not touched, let alone used by someone who did not know how it worked.) She kicked it away under the cabinet, just to be on the safe side.

Straps? No.

Heavy book? Probably not.

Marble table? Too heavy.

But, that...

Sam was dancing the tango of doom all over the sorcerer's scalp, when he caught a flash of movement out of the corner of his eye.

Quick as thought, he leapt clear, just in time to enjoy the crash as a long-legged stool, swung with a combination of strength, skill and righteous indignation, made an extremely satisfying crash into the back of the sorcerer's head.

"Gak!" said the sorcerer and collapsed to the ground.

Sam wiggled out from under the sorcerer and faced a beautiful swan maiden with fire in her eyes and a somewhat worse-for-wear stool in her hands.

He contemplated some kind of wise crack. He was sorely tempted. Then the wise, protective animal guardian side of him kicked in, and he decided that this was neither the time nor place.

"Princess Ariella" he said, bowing his head slightly but still keeping one eye firmly upon her, in case evasion became necessary "I bear greetings from your sister, Estelle. My companion and I are here to rescue you from your Unseelie captors."

Ariella thought about this for a moment, then put one hand on her hip, keeping the stool grasped firmly in the other.

"Vell, about time, it is!" she said, indignantly. "You know, I was almost having myself to rescue?

Forty-Seven
Escape, Pursuit, and a Possible Dead-End

Morgan heard footsteps in the tunnel and braced herself. She was relieved to see Sam race out of the tunnel, a woman by his side. Morgan immediately turned and looked in the direction that the guards had gone. She could still hear them thrashing about in the brush in the distance, but, as yet, they did not seem to be returning.

Sam and his companion joined her in hiding. The swan princess was tall, blond, muscular, and seemingly self-possessed, and clutched the remains of a tall stool in one hand. Given what she'd recently been through, she seemed in remarkably good shape and fine spirits.

"Any problems?" hissed Sam.

"None I couldn't handle" answered Morgan. "I managed to distract the guards and persuade them to go searching over there. It'd probably be better if we didn't wait for them to come back."

"Hello" she said, turning to the Fiederfolk woman. "I'm Morgan, and you must be Ariella."

"Vell, I guess that someone has to be," said the swan princess "and fortunate I am that I that person am. Vith you, I agree- before they are noticing that down a swan princess they are, perhaps ve should go?"

Morgan grinned. "I think I'm going to like you." she said.

"Really nice that is." said the swan woman. "but much better I think that it I would like if somevhere further away from here you liked me."

"Fair enough." said Morgan.

The three of them moved quickly away.

It hadn't taken long for the guards to find the battered and unconscious sorcerer, notice the swan princess was missing, put two and two together, and get hot on the trail of the fugitives.

Certainly not long enough.

The fugitives moved as quickly and quietly as they could, and covered as much ground as possible, but by now they could hear the sounds of pursuit coming fast behind them – dark hunds and trackers and Unseelie warriors in dismaying numbers.

Sam ran at breakneck speeds through the woods, with the women behind him. He kept a close eye on Morgan – she was in reasonably good shape, but not in training for long distance running like this. Ariella, on the other hand, was keeping up with him, although the grimace on her face told him her muscles were protesting after being immobilized for so long.

Even he couldn't outrun the dark hunds of the sidhe, and he couldn't see any way to trick them, nor any haven, save one; and that was one he didn't want to use. The portable wards were still in Morgan's purse. They were charged to keep out evil, and evil was surely what they were facing now. If he set them up and cast a circle, he could keep the creatures of the Unseelie hunt at bay for a time.

But only for a time. The wards were powerful but only held a finite amount of power. If you threw enough force against them, they would eventually collapse. Since they couldn't be moved while the circle was active and shutting down the circle eliminated any protection the wards could give them, casting the circle would tie them down in one place.

The wards were an option- an option of last resort. Wards worked well on a stronghold that people took shelter in indefinitely, but they needed to move quickly now and get to the Seelie court before the Mantelfiederfolk started a war. Movable wards might hold off Unseelie threats until help came to save them, but, as far as Sam knew, there was no help on the way. The movable wards were a protection of last resort, but, watching how Morgan was slowly falling behind, and listening to the pursuit getting closer, Sam thought last resort might be sooner rather than later.

They splashed into and across a stream, Sam guiding them upstream in the rushing water to confuse their trail. They took advantage of any rocky outcrops, as that would confuse the dark hunds as well. They twisted and wove through the underbrush, and still the sound of the pursuit behind them grew closer and closer.

They broke through a clump of trees and found themselves on the edge of a large open space with no cover to speak of. Turning back into cover would head them away from where the gates would open next, which meant the chances of war between the swan folk and the Seelie would increase; but the odds of being able to outrun dark hunds and mounted sidhe on a straightaway was small.

Still they had to try.

Clear of uneven forest ground, Sam ran flat-out, Ariella close behind him and Morgan bringing up the rear. He could see some rocks that could provide partial cover at the far side of this plain if they could to reach them before the sidhe spotted them.

Sam ran like he had never run before, and Ariella and Morgan ran after him. In a few moments, they were near the far edge of the open lands, and Sam allowed himself hope that they might actually make it into cover before their pursuers saw them.

Unfortunately, this was not the case.

The first of the dark hunds broke through the edge of the forest and saw them. A howl went up as the dog spied them, before charging across the open field towards them. The fugitives could feel pursuit coming up fast behind.

Looking back, Sam saw Morgan was losing ground, and that it wouldn't take long for the hunt to overtake her. Quick as thought, he doubled back, passing Ariella and turning to pace Morgan.

"The purse! Put it down now!" he shouted. "Ariella, to us!"

The swan princess pivoted and ran back to them, brandishing her stool leg fiercely at the oncoming canine. "A plan you had best have, cat." panted the swan as she reached them. "Another nice little visit vith those Unseelie boys I am not minded to again have, no."

The Unseelie dog was almost to them, and more were appearing at the edge of the woods. Morgan reached into her purse and pulled something out.

The first hund reached them. Teeth bared and barking wildly, he lunged at them. Morgan drew back and threw something into his open maw. Things glittered as they flew across the space and into the dog's mouth.

The hund gulped and gasped and choked. It screamed and began to paw furiously at its mouth, turning and running back towards its masters.

Sam looked at Morgan surprised. "What...?" he started.

"Thumb tacks" she replied, cutting him off as she reached into her purse again. "with steel tips. Steel's an iron alloy, I figured he wouldn't like them, and the points make them hard to get rid of."

"Now get casting." Morgan said, tossing Sam the bundle of wards. "We got more on the way, and I've used up most of my office supplies."

Sam grinned but was too busy to reply. He was running to place the wards in east, south, west and north. He had a circle to cast as ravening dark hunds bore down at them across the open plain.

Sam ran swiftly to the first crystal in the east. Reaching it, he sat in the formal cat position, head alert, paws together, back straight, ears listening, and tail wrapped carefully and formally around his paws. Once in position, he spoke.

"Guardians of the watchtowers of the east..." he began.

The first dark hund had retreated but his fellow pack members were coming. They looked backwards for a moment, baying to draw the rest of the hunt to them before loping towards the fugitives.

Morgan scattered the rest of the thumb tacks on the ground outside of the wards, concentrating on the direction the hunt was coming from.

The first point of the circle called, the golden cat rose and ran clockwise to the next crystal in the south. Once again, he assumed a posture of respect.

"Guardians of the watchtowers of the south..."

The other hunds were almost to the fugitives. There were more than a dozen of them visible now, each as large as a Great Dane; and they growled and howled and snarled as they ran.

Up and moving once again, and picking up speed as he went, Sam dashed to the west. Once more he sat respectfully and spoke.

"Guardians of the watchtowers of the west..." he cried

There was a shout at the border of the woods, as the first of the Unseelie warriors reached forest's edge and saw their prey in sight.

Sam sped madly towards the final crystal in the north, as death hurtled down on them. Reaching it, he sat as carefully as if he had all of the time in the world.

"Guardians of the watchtowers of the north, I bid you welcome and I ask for your protection now from all things evil and of darkness."

Morgan's breath caught in her throat. The dark hunds were barreling down on them, with elven warriors close behind them. Even if Sam got the circle up in time, this would only be a temporary reprieve. She reached into her purse once more and pulled out a pair of oversized heavy-duty steel office scissors

Sam made a final clockwise sprint, ending at the eastern crystal where he began. He seated himself carefully one last time.

"The circle is closed. So mote it be!" he shouted. His voice was magnified, booming across the plain like thunder.

The sound echoed out across the plain, and a circle of Light sprang up once more. Light passing from crystal to crystal. Light connecting in a circle of Light. Light forming a dome above them. Light flooding the world around them.

The dark hunds skidded to an abrupt halt, yelping piteously. The Unseelie cried out and covered their dark eyes.

Sam rose to his hind legs, pawing at Ariella's knee to get her attention. "Be sure to stay inside of the circle of Light" he said. "If we cross it, we break it, and the protection that it gives us goes down."

Ariella nodded. "Such things before I have seen" she said. "but strong enough it is? Safe how long vill ve be?"

"I don't know" said Sam, his face troubled. "But it was the only option we had left, so we'd better hope so."

The sidhe were taken aback at first, but quickly regained their courage. Dark hunds slunk across the plain more slowly, stalking the fugitives in their circle of Light. Unseelie warriors came riding up behind them on great flame-eyed steeds, lances held deceptively casually. A few dogs and lesser fae trod upon tacks and recoiled, and the rest became more cautious.

The darkling horde gathered around the circle, looking at it, poking at it. At first, the circle flared and burned with every touch, sending dark hunds yelping away with burned noses, and sidhe cursing and swearing. The circle of Light protected the fugitives, and caused their enemies pain.

Yet with every touch, every flare, the circle shone a bit less brightly, a little less radiant. Each touch, each test, drained the circle, and all too soon, the circle would go out.

And all of them could see it.

Sam looked frantically around for some final trick to play, some shelter he could send his charges to. Ariella brandished her stool leg and shouted a Mantelfieder war cry defiantly. Morgan took a firmer grip on her shears, the coolness of the steel slightly comforting given the forces they were facing.

The Unseelie sidhe laughed evilly, already rejoicing in the moment coming when the circle went down.

The circle was fading quickly under so much pressure. The Light was diminishing; and when it went out, the Unseelie forces would overwhelm them.

Forty-Eight
Diplomacy and Defense

"COME OUT!"

"COME OUT!"

"COME OUT!"

The leader of the Mantelfiederfolk had been standing in the narrow recess that led to the gates of the Seelie court and pounding on them for some time. The gates were beginning to show the strain from the ongoing assault of the angry swan shaman.

"COME OUT!"

"COME OUT!"

"COME OUT!"

Hildreth's fists were knocking on the gates, pounding on the gates, breaking down the gates with the strength of the runes held within them, while her warriors held themselves ready for the battle yet to come.

"COME OUT!"

"COME OUT!"

"COME OUT!"

The gates were held stationary, locked in place and time by the power of the Fiederfolk runes and by the will of their wielder. The gates were shuddering, trembling, quaking under the sheer force of the blows that struck them and the magick that empowered the blows. The gates were cracking, gradually splitting and splintering into pieces, subject to the inexorable attack.

And, finally, the tall gates opened.

The Mantelfiederfolk stepped back, prepared for armed resistance. The swan knights spread out, giving themselves room to maneuver.

The gates opened, and out stepped the palm reader. She was short and stout, with long brown hair and thick spectacles framing her features. She wore flowing garments, gracefully draped, with a neck full of amulets and comfortable sneakers to complete the outfit. She leaned on a staff and had a kind face that spoke of patience and inner strength.

She looked at the assembled Mantelfiederfolk with interest for a moment. "So, I hear that you have business with the Seelie court." she said mildly.

The Fiederfolk froze for a moment, finding the entire situation hard to understand. They were here in full force, a war band of the Mantelfiederfolk, in order to declare war upon the Seelie court; and the court was responding with a kitten and this small, round woman?

"Now I'm absolutely sure that the court will be glad to hear you out," the palm reader continued, "but I'm afraid that now is a very bad time for it. Can I possibly take a message for you, and have the officers of the court get back to you as soon as they can?"

Indignation swelled in every swannish heart. They had been sorely wronged! They were here to correct those wrongs! They were here to go to war to reclaim their princess and collect a wergild for each and every warrior who had died at the hands of their enemies! The Mantelfiederfolk took a collective breath in, preparing to express their anger and indignation.

Hildreth beat the rest of her people to the punch. She lunged forwards into the face of the palm reader, blustering at her as the palmist observed the swan shaman mildly.

"A message can you take!?! A message can you take!?!" Hildreth roared violently. "A casual visit this is not. A var band this is! Ve are here at the Seelie court to var declare - for our varriors, that the Seelie by deceit have slaughtered; for mein daughter, that de Seelie avay have stolen; for all of the wrongs that the Seelie unto the

208

Fiederfolk have done! Var this is, and in blood is the only vay the veregild shall be paid!"

Her fists were clenched, and her face red with anger by the time that she finished. Her people shouted in support and vigorously beat their axes upon their shields.

The palm reader continued to watch them calmly and quietly.

The uproar began to ebb. She was so calm, so quiet. Her manner was so mild that the swan people began to feel uncharacteristically self-conscious about the noise.

The palm reader waited until the noise died down. "Your princess?" she said. "I give you my solemn word that she is not here, and has not been, and that no one here has harmed her. Indeed, word has been brought to the court that she was taken by a band of Unseelie sidhe, and some of our people are out there now trying to locate her. No one of this court has harmed any of your other people either. After all, as the Mantelfiederfolk, you have a reputation as fierce warriors. Whatever else the people of this court might be, they're not usually fools; and attacking your warriors would be a foolish act indeed."

The swan folk thought for a moment about this. They were indeed a fearsome people. It surely would be foolish to take such evil actions against them, and to leave oneself open to potential reprisals. Some of them even began to nod at each other in agreement.

Their leader, however, was having none of this. "On us, your elven glamour you shall not use." Hildreth snarled. "This lie that the Unseelie are responsible ve have heard, but this proof ve have that the Seelie the villains are."

She pulled out the cloak clasp and brandished it in the face of the woman opposite her. "From our righteous wrath, your lies vill not you defend" the swan shaman shouted. "Of the evil of this court, proof ve have. Vengeance ve vill have, vengeance for the ill that your people to ours have done!"

The palm reader examined the brooch with interest.

"Yes, that certainly does look like a Seelie brooch" she said, "but your swan princess is still not here. This must be some kind of misunderstanding – the members of the Seelie court have not done these things."

"Vell, your solemn vord for it ve are not taking!" shouted Hildreth. "Your gates ve vill be knocking down, your defenses overrunning, vith your varriors severely dealing, and for our own the halls of the Seelie court taking. Then ourselves ve shall be seeing about vhether mein daughter imprisoned or dead you have; and vhether mein people you have harmed!"

There was a polite clearing of a throat behind the two women. Hildreth wheeled about quickly.

At the gate, she saw the tarot reader standing.

He was tall and strong and sturdy looking. He was dressed in metal, denim and leather, with magick sigils on his clothing, and a mass of amulets about his neck. He leaned upon a blackthorn staff, embedded with runes. His face was foreboding, under his long grey beard.

He looked at her inquiringly, saying not a word. And Hildreth paused. She suddenly felt hesitant, like she was about to drop into a pit that she hadn't noticed.

Time stood still for a moment…

Hildreth shook her head and came out of her daze. She reached back and unshipped her war axe with a fierce battle cry. Moving rapidly, she swang the axe forwards at the head of the small woman before her.

Something flashed across in front of her and stopped her axe cold.

Her muscles strained but the axe was going nowhere. It was caught in midair below the axe head by a massive black staff covered with runes marked in red. She looked up and into the mild eyes of the tarot reader, who effortlessly held her axe immobile with no signs of effort.

"Runes, eh?" he said quietly. "Well, more than one can play at that. Care to rethink this?"

Rage at fever pitch, she screamed and tore her axe loose, spinning it round at a different angle. The older man pivoted, catching her axe and deflecting it from its target. The axe sped past the palm reader and off to the side, picking up speed as it went.

The palmist ducked and pivoted out from the midst of the conflict, swinging her own lighter staff up into a ready position. Two swan guards drew hand axes and rushed in, only to be greeted with a spinning staff that seemed everywhere at once. The space was tight for them to work effectively together and what little space there was seemed full of spinning staff and humming palmist.

The swan chieftain turned, swinging her axe in from the other side. The gray man swung his staff like the wind, striking at the axe and repeatedly knocking it from its path, while never directly in the path of the blade.

The sound of impacts and the deeper breathing of the warriors in movement surged, echoing in the narrow courtyard outside of the gates. A hand axe flew through the air, caught and ripped from the hand of a swan warrior. The swan shaman's war axe was knocked aside once more, striking sparks as it struck the stone that lined the aperture.

The other swan warriors started forwards, looking for space where they could take an active part in the battle. Suddenly there was a shriek and a rush of air, and a winged kitten was amongst them, darting at eyes and necks.

The palmist blocked a hand axe. The tarot reader deflected the swan shaman's axe again, and their eyes met briefly through the chaos.

The palmist reached up and seized the kitten as he darted by, flicking him vigorously back through the big oaken gates. The man and women shouted as one and then leaped backwards through the gates, slamming them closed and barring them.

Panting, they leaned back against the gates, feeling the sounds of pounding begin once again. At their feet, an indignant kitten bristled and complained about how he was a warrior and didn't deserve such treatment.

"I could have taken them…" the tarot reader said.

"Yes, I know," the palmist soothed "but we have sick people to tend."

Behind them, the pounding began again.

Forty-Nine
An Unexpected Rescue

It is fitting that a war band rides hard and fast. There are places they must be and things they must do, and the more quickly they can be and do them, the better the chances of success. In a nomadic society, this often means splitting the flock; sending the bulk of the fastest, most powerful warriors to ride ahead and secure new territory, while the old, the young and those who care for both are left to pack, and follow more slowly, guarded by other warriors. Many times, these warriors include the fiercest and most competent, for every warrior fights more fiercely, knowing that family and flock are safely guarded.

So it was in this case. Hildreth rode for the Seelie court with a fierce group of Fiederfolk warriors, but she left others behind to guard the flock while they packed the camp and brought it along more slowly. This group of wagons, warriors, and families was steadily making its way towards the rendezvous, when a lone outrider spotted something curious in the distance. A group of dark hunds and savage looking sidhe had surrounded two women, and were stalking around and around them, for no reason that the scout could see. Given the small amount of opposition, why did they not simply overrun them?

Unexplained things can sometimes cause trouble for folks passing by. Wanting to know if this situation was a threat and also being curious, the scout signaled to one of the aerial sentries.

When on the move, some swan knights ride on horseback, ready to face a direct threat. Others don swan skins and take to the air, spying out the best routes and possible problems to avoid before the flock comes near. Each has signals to co-ordinate with the other.

213

The aerial scout took over from the ground rider, winging his way closer to the Unseelie to see if he could find out what was happening and what would be the best response for his flock below. He came in fast and at an angle, doing his best to avoid spears or arrows while still getting a closer look at the situation. When he got closer, he was astonished to see Ariella, the missing swan princess, trapped with another woman and a small animal in the midst of a seething mass of Unseelie.

As with any swan knight, his reaction was fearless and immediate. Without hesitation, he altered his angle of flight, barreling in towards the fight like a diving eagle in a rage. As he dove, he trumpeted three times.

His fellows in the camp train heard the call to arms and looked up to see him disappearing below the tree line. They immediately changed course to follow his angle of the descent, those in human form unsheathing weapons and falling into formation, those in swan form pulling into a powerful wedge before following their scout. Even the camp wagons fell in behind, grey beards bringing their weapons to readiness and cygnets fingering knives.

Ariella, Morgan and Sam stood braced within the wards, waiting for the final rush. The dark hunds had been testing those wards for some time and had become bolder as they gradually weakened. The sidhe were also growing bolder. The swan princess still clutched the remains of the stool, but courage and a stool leg did not seem enough to deal with what now faced them.

The Unseelie hunt lord was feeling confident. A moment or two more and the wards would finally fail. They would recapture the prisoner, and two more besides. No one was looking up; which is why everyone was startled when the massive swan dove into their midst.

The swan knight landed forcibly and immediately

went to work. He hissed like a cobra. He struck at the warriors with his wings, fierce blows that did grievous damage and broke bones. He savagely bit, inflicting great wounds. He trumpeted wildly. He rose slightly into the air and flew into their faces, blinding them and battering them with his feathers.

The Unseelie, a minute before almost smug in their triumph, were now sorely undone. They cried out. They screamed. They ran to and fro, overcome with panic, fear and pain. The dark hunds howled and ran, ears flat and tails tucked firmly between their legs.

"That is very satisfying" said Sam, observing.

Ariella was too busy to answer. She had stepped out of the wards and was vigorously applying the leg of the stool to any Unseelie opportunity.

Amidst the chaos, the Unseelie leader gathered himself together and draw his weapon. No big bird was going to overcome him! He strode towards the swan knight, sword at the ready.

"Watch out!"" cried Morgan, as he neared the swan.

The swan knight's head whipped about almost 180 degrees on its long and flexible neck. His body quickly followed.

Everything went still for a moment (except for Ariella still cracking heads in the back ground.)

The sidhe looked at the swan. The swan looked at the sidhe. Time hesitated, as they braced for combat.

And then the rest of the Mantelfiederfolk poured into the area and ground the Unseelie into the earth...

Sam braced himself upright on the pommel of the rapidly moving horse, riding in front of the Fiederfolk warrior.

"This is so much faster than walking!" he shouted to Morgan, on the next horse over from him.

"It is" she shouted back, "but I hope that it's fast enough to get us there in time. The Fiederfolk have been deceived and, if we don't get there soon, terrible things might happen."

"True enough" shouted Sam. "Faster then, my friend, if you please," said the cat, looking up at the massive swan warrior.

The swan knight smiled. He had heard what the cat had done for his princess.

"As you vish, mein liddle varrior friend" said the swan knight.

Fifty
The Truth

Outside of the gates, the swan folk were readying for war. Their chieftain was pounding fiercely, wood warping under the force of her blows. The warriors shouted war cries and readied themselves to make best use of the confined space when the gates finally went down.

Inside, palmist and tarot reader braced themselves against the doors, reinforcing them with their bodies and what magic they could. The gates held for now but they would not last indefinitely.

In the distance, they all heard the sound of a horn blowing and horses and wagons approaching.

Hildreth shook off her doubts.

"The rest of mein flock now comes, the Seelie halls to take!" she crowed. "Now, for the evil to us done, justice ve shall have!"

The horses of the swan knights poured over the hill and down the road the eleven gates were located on, wagons close behind them. Human and elven lands overlapped for a moment. Somehow, humans moved aside for the swans, not noticing their fantastic neighbors.

"Just in time!" Hildreth cried to her arriving wedgemates. "just in time, here you are to see justice done, judgement passed, and those villains who have wronged our people the price in blood pay."

The riders parted, revealing the non- swans who rode with them. Morgan threw herself off a horse, and ran to the gates, Sam hot at her heels.

"Noble leader of the Mantelfiederfolk," she gasped "the Seelie court is innocent of these evil deeds. We have brought proof to you that this is so."

"You again, eh?" growled the swan shaman "Vell,

217

as before I have said, proof ve also have – proof of Seelie villainy. Ve do not belief vhat you say."

"Them you do not believe. Me vill you believe?" said a new figure sliding down off of a horse.

Shocked, the swan warriors fell silent. The energy changed, and the palmist, sensing this, opened the gate a sliver to peek out. She then opened it wider and stepped outside once more, trailed by her husband.

Hildreth saw Ariella – ruffled and bruised looking, but definitely her eldest daughter, walking towards her with her younger sister Estelle running to join her. The leader of the swan people stared, mind racing in an attempt to take this in.

Her daughter was safe. She had given up hope of that.

"Mother, not by the Seelie court vas I taken. By a band of the Unseelie, this evil was done." said Ariella emphatically. "In mein abduction and the death of our varriors, blameless the Seelie are."

The swan shaman stood thunderstruck, adjusting to this new situation "But this brooch…" she stammered "vit your bloodstained feather cloak, this Seelie brooch ve found …"

Ariella looked at the brooch and shook her head. "Of that, I do not know" she said "Trying to deceive us perhaps someone was. I only know that Unseelie my captors were - and more than that, that mein freedom and mein life itself to this voman and her cat I owe. In mein hour of need, me they came to rescue. You should not them disregard. A debt to them you owe."

"Now who vill you believe?" Ariella said to her mother. "A foolish piece of jewelry- or your daughter?"

In a moment, the anger of the swan shamaness fell out from beneath her, leaving her feeling uncertain. She had been so sure that the facts told one story. It was hard to change those beliefs.

She had almost made a terrible mistake.

Slowly, she gathered herself together and adjusted to the new facts before her. She took a deep breath and found her center. After a moment, she turned back to Morgan and to the others facing her in front of the gates.

"De Mantelfiederfolk, a strong and honorable folk are." Hildreth began painfully "One part of being strong and honorable is admitting ven wrong you have been."

"And the case here, this is– wrong I vas. Mein pain and anger I almost let me lead into something horrible doing -going to var vith those who no wrong to me and mine had done."

She swallowed deeply. "For mein wrongdoing, vill you me forgive?" she asked Morgan softly.

It was Morgan's turn to take a deep breath and find her center. "Yes, of course" she said slowly. "They deceived you. I'm only glad that we could find your daughter in time."

"Is there any way that we can help you?" said the palmist. "The Seelie court did not do these things, but they would be willing to help you find out who has."

"That probably won't be necessary" said Morgan. "When the Fiederfolk warriors found us and drove off our attackers, they took prisoners."

"And here one now is" said Ariella, pushing a bound and blindfolded Unseelie sidhe forwards. "and news for us about vere ve can find his fellows, I think that he may have.

A collective growl broke loose from the lips of the assembled warriors of the Mantelfiederfolk. The Unseelie prisoner could not see them, but still quailed behind his blindfold.

Hildreth turned back to the guardians at the Gates.

"Between our peoples, now good all is," she said "Ve must ourselves excuse. Ve have business about to be."

As one, the Fiederfolk leapt into their saddles, Hildreth's first in command taking their Unseelie prisoner onto his horse before him.

As the swan folk turned and rode away, Morgan and Sam could hear the swan shaman starting to ask some hard questions.

Sam looked at Morgan. Morgan looked at Sam.

"Well, he's in for an interesting afternoon" said Sam.

"And, speaking of interesting afternoons" said the palmist, looking meaningfully at her husband "the members of the court are beginning to turn the corner, but we still have a plague spell to deal with before any significant healing can begin…"

The tarot reader twinkled at her. "…and what fun it will be to turn that spell back on the person who sent it." he said happily.

Fifty-One
Home Again

The plague had finally subsided, the first few members of the Seelie court still shaky but back on their feet, and Morgan and Sam were finally back at home and comfortable, scarred door locked and porch lights on.

They had company.

Ariella was looking through the freezer and had just discovered the wonders of ice cream. The winged kitten was exploring the kitchen, and Sam was keeping an eye on him to make sure that he didn't get into trouble or help himself to any treats that were Sam's by right.

And Estelle was sitting quietly in the side chair, staring into space, her face blank.

Morgan was the first to notice. "Are you o.k., Estelle?" she asked, sitting down next to her. "You seem a little quiet."

Estelle blinked, and turned to look at her. She took a deep breath. "Just thinking, I vas," she began slowly. "just thinking about the svan knights who beyond have passed."

There was suspicious moisture at the corners of her eyes. She looked so sad that Morgan wanted to hold her, but she wasn't sure about how Estelle felt about that.

Ariella had no such hesitation, plumping down in the chair on the other side of her sister and wrapping an arm around her. "Sad it is," she said more seriously. "So many svan knights gone. Glad I am that I alive I am, and that var ve have avoided, but sorry too for the svans that ve have lost."

"The faces gone." said Estelle "The friends that ve shall never in this vorld again see."

They sat in remembrance for a moment.

"And, vorse yet, over I do not think this is." the younger swan maiden whispered, her eyes blank.

The room went still and the hair stood up on the back of Morgan's neck. Estelle had inherited the skills of a shaman. At that point, her instincts were worth heeding.

Sam padded across the room and sat at Estelle's feet. He looked up into her eyes for a moment and then climbed up into her lap.

"You know, you're right about that" he said softly. "As long as we're on this earth, the story doesn't end. Trouble may come- but you know what?"

"Nein." she said quietly

"If trouble comes" said the cat "we'll deal with it. We'll deal with it because someone has to and sometimes that someone is us. We'll deal with it because that's how we roll."

He smiled at her and, in a moment, she smiled back.

"Now will somebody with thumbs open the fridge for me?" the golden cat said more loudly. "I'm not sure, but I think there may be some tuna sashimi in there and heroes need energy."

"Especially the handsome four-legged kind." he added as he leapt to the floor.

The tension broke and they all laughed in relief. Morgan followed her roommate into the kitchen and the others trailed after her.

Fifty- Two
Analysis

"Well, that did not go as expected" the Unseelie lord thought morosely, toying with his goblet. He'd had a hard few days, fighting off the effects of his plague spell turned back upon him.

"My plan should have worked. It should have debilitated the Seelie court, pitted the Seelie against the swan folk, and left both sides weak and open to an Unseelie takeover."

Restless, he stood up and paced the length of his shadowy workroom.

"It should have worked… but for some reason, it did not."

He took another draft from his goblet, and suddenly angry, threw it to the floor in the corner. "Why did it not work?" he raged. "It should have worked! It was a perfect plan! If not for that incompetent sorcerer being not anywhere as powerful as he claimed to be, and the princess getting loose, and the Seelie refusing to fight, and that stupid woman and her cat, they would have torn each other to pieces and I would be sitting on the throne right now."

"It was perfect… but it still did not work."

His eyes narrowed, and, as suddenly as he had raged, he was ice cold again.

"Of course, there is always next time "he thought. "I will just have to do better next time."

And he began to think again…

Glossary

Banshee- spirit whose wailing warns of impending death.

Brownie – small sidhe who makes himself responsible for the place he lives and comes out at night to do chores.

Cob – a male swan.

Cygnet- a young swan.

Dan tien- Dantien are qi focus flow centers, important focal points for meditative and exercise techniques such as qigong, martial arts such as tai chi, and in traditional Chinese medicine.

Dark hund- large Unseelie hound.

Ether/Aether- energy that occupies the space between all things.

Fae- another term for Sidhe or fairy folk.

Glamour- illusion often used by the fae.

Hearth spirit- protective spirit of a home.

Hob- general name for a tribe of kindly, beneficent and occasionally mischievous spirits. A Brownie is one type of hob.

Mantelfieder- the special feathered cloak used by the swan people to transform from their human form to the form of a swan.

Mantelfiederfolk- the swan people.

Qigong - an ancient Chinese healing art involving meditation, controlled breathing, and movement exercises.

Seelie- those of the sidhe considered to be more beneficent or at least benign to humans.

Sidhe- a shortened form of aos sidhe, a term for the fairy People.

Unseelie- those of the sidhe considered to be more actively malevolent towards humans.

Warding- a method of protecting a space from negative

energies or beings.

Ward- objects used to anchor the energy of warding in a place.

Wergild (or as Hildreth puts it "Vergild")- the value set in Anglo-Saxon and Germanic law upon human life in accordance with rank and paid as compensation to the kindred or lord of a slain person.

This book is dedicated to

Morgan Daimler

Who loaned me her name at a critical time,

And whose polite but persistent inquiries about the fate of her namesake is one of the reasons that this book exists.

It is good for writers to be in the company of other writers

Acknowledgements

And we're back to the Lands that Lie Between again. I'll be your guide but there's a lot of other important people who made this trip possible.

Many thanks to Morgan, Tchipakkan, Carol and Gini, who pitched in in an assortment of useful ways with the usual ridiculously short deadlines. Whether it's brainstorming, editing, giving feedback, gently nagging me or reading and commenting while sick, you ladies are the bomb and this story wouldn't be what it is without you all.

My gratitude to all of my fellow writers for encouragement, inspiration, support and kindness, and for getting me writing again after a long dry spell. A writer needs a tribe.

Thanks to my friends who gave permission for me to use their mannerisms and appearances as models for some of my characters. (No, they're still not you, but there's a hint of you in them…)

Love and gratitude to my family and friends, who've encouraged my writing since I was very small (and continue to do so, even though I'm still only fun sized.)

My thanks to all of the folks who've read my other books and have been politely nudging me to get this one out into the world. This one's for you.

And most of all to my husband Starwolf, whose love, patience and support continue to make my writing possible. Every story needs a hero, and you're mine.

Catherine Kane was raised by feral storytellers. She is a teller of tales, a poet, a wordsmith and a song wright, an artist, an enthusiastic student of the Universe, a maker of very bad puns and a medieval re-enactor who spends a fair amount of time at renaissance faires when she isn't hunched over her computer, writing.

She's also a bit of an over-achiever.

Want to know more about her?

Find her on Facebook at https://www.facebook.com/Catherine-Kane-Writes/134304556668759